More by the Author

The Reztap Chronicles

Book Zero
Mishaps and Mayhem

Book One
The Adventures of Reztap

Book Two
The Quest for the Insane Moth

THE CHRONICLES OF REZTAP
BOOK ONE

THE ADVENTURES OF REZTAP

ARTEMUS WITHERS

BLUE FORGE PRESS
Port Orchard, Washington

The Adventures of Reztap
Copyright 2015, 2022
by Artemus Withers

First eBook Edition November 2018
First Print Edition November 2018
Second Print Edition April 2022

Cover art by Jerrica Law
Interior design by Brianne DiMarco

ISBN 978-1-59092-966-7

For information about film, reprint or other subsidiary rights, contact: blueforgegroup@gmail.com

Blue Forge Press is the print division of the volunteer-run, federal 501(c)3 nonprofit company, Blue Forge Group, founded in 1989 and dedicated to bringing light to the shadows and voice to the silence. We strive to empower storytellers across all walks of life with our four divisions: Blue Forge Press, Blue Forge Films, Blue Forge Gaming, and Blue Forge Records. Find out more at www.BlueForgeGroup.org

Blue Forge Press
7419 Ebbert Drive Southeast
Port Orchard, Washington 98367
blueforgepress@gmail.com
360-550-2071 ph.txt

DEDICATION

To my grandfather, who kept his life honorable and always looked out for his family. We wouldn't be here today if it weren't for you. I wouldn't be the man I am today without your example. A husband, father, grandfather, police officer, entrepreneur, mason, and horse enthusiast, he will always hold a special place in my heart.

ACKNOWLEDGEMENTS

My main goal with this book and the ones coming after is to entertain, make you smile and maybe even laugh. I honestly think the world is a better place if we can laugh... just not while we're torturing a prisoner or something heinous.

This book has been a long time in the making. It started out from the smallest kernel—the word Reztap—and has grown into this diamond of a book. (Maybe it's really cubic zirconia, but I won't tell if you don't.)

If you enjoy snappy, comedic space opera, you should enjoy this book. I get my inspiration from the likes of Douglas Adams, Harry Harrison, Joss Whedon, Robert Aspirin and Terry Pratchett. As with many authors, there's a lot of "me" in the writing, the characters and the message. Just think of all the good parts as me and all the bad parts as additions to balance it all out.

I would like to thank my best friend, James Patterson, who granted me the name Reztap when we were in middle school. Another childhood friend, William Taylor, was the inspiration for Gorth. My crazy upbringing provided the framework for many of the eccentricities in Tar's life, but certainly not all of them. Chuck is really an innocent child inspired by all the people I've met in life. As with all children, they grow up and are influenced by factors beyond their control.

My wife, Dawn, and children, Jessica, Robyn and Nikki, are the real framework of my life. I truly owe them a debt of gratitude for their support in my insane aspiration to become a published writer. They also stuck with me through my days with the improv troupe and they never wavered in their support. To my mother, Gail, I owe my life in more ways than one. To my sisters, Dana and Jeannette, I owe my grounding in reality. They've been through so much and come out incredibly strong. I'm inspired by their strength and resolve every day.

To my awesome cover artist, Jerrica Law—you put life into Tar and Gorth and made me smile from ear to ear when I saw the cover art!

Biggest thanks to all of you—the readers. Without readers, writers are merely crazy people writing in a corner, dribbling and babbling incoherently to no one. Thank you for letting me babble to you!

THE CHRONICLES OF REZTAP
BOOK ONE

THE ADVENTURES OF REZTAP

ARTEMUS WITHERS

CHAPTER 1
PORT WHINE

A simple plan should be easy to execute with a simple, yet positive outcome. With our plans, however, there were always unforeseen complications.

I was closing in on my high score in holographic ping pong when my hard work was interrupted by the inevitable whining of my best friend, Tar.

"Do you realize we've been waiting over an hour to get our berthing assignment?"

"An hour, really? Shocking," I replied and tried to ignore his incessant rambling to no avail. As he paced the length of the bridge, his face contorted into the best scowl he could manage. I admired his earnest effort to appear menacing, but at five feet, six inches with a slender build, he appeared childlike in comparison to my decidedly larger frame.

"I spent the first half of my life working my fingers to the bone just to get a permit to berth the Namreg here, and they have the gall to make me wait over an hour for an assignment. All that sweat and money for this kind of treatment!" Tar looked ready to pull his curly brown locks out of his head.

"It is just a standard docking license, after all," I reminded him as I scratched my chin. I realized I forgot to shave this morning, feeling the slightest hint of stubble on my dark skin. I glanced at Tar and saw his five-day old scraggly beard growth and relaxed. As long as I was standing next to Tar, no one was likely to notice my shaving shortcoming.

"It's equivalent to a ransom for an entire continent on some planets. Do you know how many times I went out mining in Alpha Centauri's giant asteroid belt, instead of going on dates?" Tar stopped in front of me and folded his arms. I wrinkled my nose as I noticed he had not changed into a new jumpsuit again.

"It was in the thousands, wasn't it?" I said and smiled. He shook his head at me and resumed pacing.

"It's not funny, Gorth. I missed countless birthday parties to go frundle harvesting on Melarta. Remember Grizelda Noonig? I missed her birthday and she wanted me there. She wanted me there real bad! So, I went frundle harvesting and she took a liking to 'Kelnick the Merciless.'"

"You prevented Melarta from being overrun by frundles. That's a very noble and worthwhile cause."

Tar stopped pacing and faced me again. "I developed an allergy to the little hairballs and have you been listening to anything I've said? She wanted me, Gorth!"

"You were only nine years old," I said as I leaned my head back and resumed my game, pushing the performance envelope in holographic ping pong playing out on the ceiling.

"That's not the point. The point is that she married

Kelnick and I married this ship." Tar's blue eyes flashed as he carried on his favorite tirade. "After all that sacrifice, you'd think the scum running this place would give me a little respect and a lot better service!"

I wondered in patient silence if Tar was going to include the number of times he'd gone bounty hunting for throggles in the throggle-plagued Halfaantrin system, missing all the independence celebrations on his home planet, Andros. Not that missing them was horrible to anyone except his upper crust family embroiled in the political affairs and operations there; it would look bad if he didn't attend. He was more than eager to avoid complications with his mother. Few punishments in the galaxy were more stinging than her wrath.

"I went bounty hunting for Throggles and..."

"Namreg, you are cleared for approach," a monotone female voice announced over the speakers.

"About time!"

I ended my game and engaged the automated docking procedure. Our giant yellow ship slinked past the guard post. Through our external video feed, I observed the guard watching in stunned silence as she glided by. Past experience gave me an idea of what was going through his limited intellect. I imagined he looked at the general construction of the behemoth and wondered how we got a permit to fly it in space. Our unconventional trader resembled a glob of mashed potatoes suspended in zero gravity—she was large with a unique and unconventional design.

"The Bloated Namreg," Tar said as he observed technicians on the assembled catwalks stop what they were doing and watch as we passed. "I'm certain it's the ugliest ship they've ever seen."

As I monitored the ship's progress, Tar connected the ship's system to the dockyard's computer for a roll of ships there. As the list scrolled through the data, his eyebrows furrowed and he rubbed his forehead.

"Dryad Syndicate... we were never implicated there," Tar mumbled.

"Well placed bribes can be a godsend."

"Mychondra settlement has a government vessel... where we..."

"Paid the fines. Other charges dropped," I said. Tar nodded and began to chew nervously on his thumbnail.

The ship's virtual gyroscope rotated to the left as the Namreg arced then straightened and proceeded to her berthing assignment.

Tar's eyebrows rose. "Vymaxian warships... have we?"

"Not to my knowledge. That's a sector of space we've never been in."

A smile erupted on Tar's face.

"Sweet! Somewhere we could hide!"

"Not really. They tolerate outsiders about as well as you tolerate shaving."

Tar's lifted his hand and rubbed his stubble.

"We could go in disguise..."

"They're amphibians," I said and furrowed my brow.

Tar tapped a few times on the screen and the picture of a green, scaly face materialized. He cocked his head and examined it.

"It's not so bad."

"They live in water. I'm not permanently wrinkling my epidermis so you can feel comfortably safe from prosecution."

"We could wear suits," Tar said as he raised a

finger to the sky.

"No. I'd rather seek refuge with your parents."

Tar wrinkled his nose. "We need to have a lot more death bounties on our heads to warrant that. I think we'd be better off at your family's residence."

My mind wandered to our last visit, Tar's shenanigans and my one and only experience with the global security forces on my home planet. He was not visiting Terra again.

"My family would put you in chains after our last sojourn there."

"Yeah, well, that's infinitely better than staying with my family-"

Tar's eyes darted to me and then back to the screen.

"What is it?"

"Progorian warship at number 532."

I jumped out of my seat and scanned the list on Tar's display.

"How long have they been here?"

Tar tapped the display. "Three hours."

I released a slow breath and returned to my seat.

"No problem then. Knowing the Progorians, they're all drunk and holed up at the Courtesan Academy by now."

Tar nodded. "That should give us plenty of time."

Tar reached the bottom of the list. As he blinked at the list, his face went pale.

"Uh," he murmured as his eyes darted over to me. I tried to concentrate on the docking calculations on my screen. Tar tapped a few more times and looked over the results.

"Still, we'll want to get this done as quickly as possible. Within a couple hours, those drunken Progorians will be back on the ship looking to shoot something, and we make a mighty tempting target."

Ever vigilant to Tar's attempts to hide the truth, I stopped my calculations and looked at him.

"We probably have over twenty-four hours. They have a high level of tolerance for wicked brew."

Tar nodded.

"Right! Just trying to err on the side of caution."

I jumped out of my seat and ran to look at his display. Tar erred plenty, but rarely with caution in mind. Women, cars, and exotic animals immediately sprang to the forefront of the list—mostly wrecking them, inducing their early demise or breaking their hearts with ill-conceived schemes. He hadn't killed any women yet... except for that unfortunate incident at the recycling plant years ago.

I sighed when I saw the ship listed there.

"Fantastic." I clapped Tar on the back. "Err on the side of caution? Want to retreat now, or take our chances?"

Tar turned off the display. "Maybe it's just a coincidence and we'll be fine if we make this quick."

"Coincidence? Yeah and there's a Corrocan Rhododendron growing out of my anus."

Tar stood. He folded his arms and placed his right hand on his chin. He paced as he spoke.

"We'll turn around. Leave now," Tar said.

"He'd follow and a Republic warship doesn't have to clear customs."

"We haven't docked yet, we could make it through customs fairly quickly. Maybe he's not on board."

"It's his flagship. He's the commander. How likely is it your brother won't be on board?"

Tar stopped. He plopped down in his chair.

"Half-brother. Throw me a crumb here."

"Well, we might get bread crumbs when we're

locked up in the brig."

The ship shuddered as it completed docking.

I stood up, and we walked out of the bridge.

"Let's make this quick. Maybe he's asleep at the wheel."

I stopped and turned to Tar.

"Or sleeping off his last gargantuan meal. That, at least, has a speck of probability to it."

The main computer alarm beeped and we both turned around. I hastened back into the bridge, Tar at my heels. The monitors on the bridge of the Namreg glowed with the message:

"Reztap has arrived, heading down on shuttle 2297."

Then the monitors went blank. I quickly keyed in a trace command to no avail.

"Transmission destination unknown, but I can guess where it went."

"It's a good bet he knows we're here now. When we get back, it would be nice if you'd track down the ghost in the machine and smash it with a digital club."

We exited the large yellow ship in haste, entering the sealed walkway to the main causeway. I wished Tar's sibling nemesis was otherwise occupied and we could at least pick up our new navigator before he waylaid us. Minutes later, we were aboard space dock shuttle 2297 heading down to Selatarn. I took a deep breath. Positive thoughts and meditation should help us prepare for what waited below. It never worked before, but there was always a first time.

Chapter 2
A Flashy Exit

Selatarn, the economic capital of the known universe, spread out across the encapsulated atmosphere dome before us. Every major business in the galaxy had at least an office here if not their company headquarters on this gargantuan asteroid. Political representatives from thousands of solar systems held court in the vibrant political and economic playground. The number of living bodies in this location made it the ideal place to search for the live navigator we desperately sought—a classic case of high demand and low supply especially for us.

We walked down the main avenue on the sun side of the enormous space rock. Here, custom-made optical inhibitors diffused the direct sunlight. I glanced around, noting that most inhabitants wore sunglasses anyway. Bright solar rays reflected an array of colors off of the multi-colored buildings. Moist, recycled air behaved like millions of tiny prisms creating an omnipresent rainbow in the sky. We fought our way through the crowded walkways, taking more time than we'd anticipated reaching our destination, Galloper's Interstellar Bar and Grille.

The contours of the star-shaped structure before us gave away its age. The curve of the roof suggested early pioneer constructions found only here on Selatarn, while the milky appearance of the walls reminded me of a gentler era—one when beauty won out over making a buck.

A familiar and unmistakable odor of vomit, smoke and the sweat of a hundred different galactic species reminded me this remained a popular hangout for the filthiest inhabitants of the universe. Tar sucked in a deep breath of the discolored air around us. He choked on the cloud of funk, coughing and spitting to clear his mouth and lungs of the obnoxious air particles infiltrating them.

"You going to make it?" I asked.

Tar gave me a silent thumbs up as his breathing calmed and he took smaller breaths. It had been a long time since our last visit and Tar must've forgotten the usual sights and smells.

"Galloper's," Tar stated. "Founded by Quentin Galloper nearly a century ago. Quentin Galloper, the most successful trader of all time!"

"Tar, Quentin Galloper was a cheat, a criminal, and a scoundrel."

"Don't ruin this moment with facts, Gorth. Savor the atmosphere."

"I'm already there."

A smoky stench filled the air inside Galloper's. The classic haunt's high, domed ceilings resembled a great hall. These days it had become a place for the smoke and excreted biological gasses to coalesce and further diffused already dim lighting. Vintage design no longer attracted people to Galloper's. Customers came to make deals, meet people and arrange crimes.

A vicious clamor rose out of the crowd, a melody of murmurs, cries, grunts, and groans, accompanied by tones of a tenor being tortured somewhere. Tar ducked as laser blasts erupted from the southern wing where a disgruntled poker player charred a large portion of the crowd before someone finally blew his arm off. In another wing, a meeting of the local assassins' guild got lively. The rest of the bar patrons gave them space. Nobody wanted to deal with an angry assassin. All in all, it was a relatively tame day for Galloper's.

Suddenly, an exuberant cry sliced through the oppressive gloom. "Hey, everyone, it's Tar Reztap!"

Except for an enthusiastic sneeze from a Polarian Dustsucker, there was no reaction from the customers. However, the young man who uttered the cry jumped and waved at us. Tar's eyes darted around until he found an empty bottle that he broke over the youth's disheveled mess of vibrant red hair.

"Maybe next time he'll think twice about making my presence known before I'm ready. Little loud-mouth ruined my entrance," Tar said as he wiped his hands off on his pants.

"Theoretically, your planned entrance could have been enhanced by the emotional fervor of that young adolescent, had you capitalized on the event," I said.

Tar stared at me for a few seconds. He began to speak, then stopped himself.

"What?"

"Never mind, Gorth. Forget it."

Tar strolled toward the darkest, smelliest, and most pernicious booth available and pointed. I nodded at his choice. I deposited the formerly enthusiastic young man's limp body into the booth. The resounding thud was accentuated by a high-pitched squeak from a bedraggled tenor, rather upset at having a limp body dumped on him, what with his being recently mugged and all. After the tenor steadied himself on the table, he lectured me on the common courtesy normally observed for fresh mugging victims. I opened my mouth to apologize, but was immediately cut off by the irate and surprisingly loud singer standing before me. Although I could easily knock the small man into orbit with a swipe of my huge hand, I waited for him to finish with a patience belying my intimidating features.

I attempted to speak once more, but the man interrupted me.

"You have the inferior intellect of a small time burglar and likely the same sized manhood!" he said. I blinked and blushed. Where did this peaceful-looking man pick up such a colorful vocabulary?

"In all likelihood, your parents met at a bar and you're the object of a mistaken, drunken night of off note debauchery!"

I cocked my head at the delirious or perhaps drunken man. His mouth may be what had gotten him pummeled in the first place. I had my doubts that he'd been mugged at all.

"I bet your parents couldn't carry a tune any better than they splice genetic material to create such disappointing offal as yourself." The man stumbled a bit after the last bit. I was pretty sure he was winding down.

"I think you mean offspring, but I-"

"Oh, do I now?" The man brought all of his diminutive five foot tall stature to bear as he tripped into my chest with his face and stared up at me.

"You're the type of Terran viscera that makes me vomit! Descended from primates? More likely descended from slugs!"

The man's breath smelled of alcohol, vomit and three-day-old gym socks. I felt pity for anyone smelling his breath and also for his own tongue and teeth. I was going to just push him gently back down onto a chair until he leaped into a vivid description of me performing a sexual act with a slime-oozing witzel. The witzel is the lowest of invertebrates on a near dead frontier world that procreate by suffocating their mates and absorbing genetic material through their skin. They then split like an amoeba and become four creatures of the new genetic combination. That I would subscribe myself to such a mating and death to further my genetic influence on a dark world with no semblance of social or technological structure pushed me over the limit. I balled my fist and hit the man firmly on the chin. Consciousness picked this moment to take a holiday from the vulgar mouthed singer and he collapsed with the second resounding thud of the day, landing on top of the young man Tar rendered unconscious a few minutes earlier. I dusted my hands off and decided I needed to find Tar.

After a brief search, I found him at the bar.

"How's the kid?" Tar asked as I sat down.

"Slumbering painfully," I said.

"Two of whatever Galloper's is peddling these days," Tar told the bartender.

"Two Altarian Algae Ales?"

Tar nodded and then turned his attention back to me. "You were saying?"

The bartender set two frosted glass steins on the wooden counter in front of us. I looked warily at the thick, green liquid and took a sip. The green froth touched my lips and my stomach constricted. I pushed the green drink as far away as I could without leaving my chair.

"It can't be that bad," Tar said with a smirk. He took a swig of his ale and promptly choked on it. He slid his glass next to mine. "What in the world is in there? And who would pay for it?"

I laughed. "'Can't be that bad,'" I mimicked. Tar ignored me.

"Have you seen Tob anywhere in here? I know you're just as anxious to leave Galloper's as I am."

"I haven't seen him, but someone has seen us." I tapped Tar on the shoulder and pointed to our left.

Tar turned around to see a black-armored individual wielding a small, but dangerous, military laser cannon. He beckoned us to follow with an insistent wave of the deadly weapon. I knew what was coming next and closed my eyes as I saw Tar raising his hands to the sky. I counted to three and dropped to my knees as I heard a shout of surprise from in front of us and saw the bit of blinding light that made it through my closed eyelids. I felt Tar's hand grasp my jumpsuit collar and I opened my eyes. Our assailant had his eyes clasped shut, holding them with one hand and firing ahead in a barely discernible pattern. After a few seconds, I realized where our moment of opportunity to escape was and grabbed Tar's arm. We made our way out of the crowd and back out the front entrance. Sure enough, there were two military goons there with weapons at the ready. Tar raised his hands again and I shut my eyes. This blinding technique was a new one we'd never utilized before. I wondered how long the surprise would be effective. The two guards fired blindly at the front of Galloper's and we hastily made our exit south into the bustling throng of alien life that teemed in the asteroid's thoroughfare.

"Tar," I said as I worked to save the wares of vendors Tar was jostling in his attempt to escape. "You know how this is going to end."

"What we are doing, my friend," Tar said as I grabbed a cart of Nilothian Tickle Worms he nearly upended, "is making him think twice before simply dispatching his goons after us again. Are we worth the trouble? Would the bad will generated by his blast-happy agents be worth the very not-hassle-free engagement of my services?"

I dodged a flock of Feathered Artificers upset by our passing. I didn't need a fancy hat generated on my head while running for my freedom. Then again...

I grabbed two of the floating robots and slapped one on Tar's head and the other on my own as I pulled him into an alley. Tar kept silent as he searched for our pursuers through a bushel of blood fronds. As we waited patiently for a little over three minutes, the textile robots went to work fashioning a concealing cloak from head to foot for both of us.

"They've donned goggles," Tar said as the Feathered Artificers finished the bottom hem of the robes. They beeped incessantly until Tar waved his arm past them, signaling a sale with his sub-dermal credit chip and an inaudible guttural vibration from his throat. The two automated clothiers beeped happily and then shot up into the air trilling loudly to announce they'd made a sale. That was exactly the last thing we needed. Every pursuer within earshot looked at the two flying globes and immediately began to converge on the estimated beginning of their exuberant arc.

"Great," I murmured. We both looked at the dead end alley behind us. I winced, but the cloak covered my face so no one could see it. Tar grabbed my arm and we ventured further into our cornered enclosure. I looked behind us. No one had reached the entrance to the alley yet. As I turned back around, I noted Tar had seen a camouflaged doorway I hadn't noticed from afar. He began to examine the edges. There was no handle on the exterior; I figured it was an emergency exit only door. I looked up at the building and a thought tickled the back of my mind.

"Uh, maybe we should just surrender," I said as a feeling of apprehension weighed on me like a blanket soaked in Arcturan dung.

"No way," Tar said. His fingers rubbed over a spot several times and he nodded. He dug under the robe and pulled out a pocket knife. "Sometimes the simplest tool is all you need to gain your freedom!"

Tar slid the knife into the slot and I heard a click. The door popped open with a slight hiss. He grabbed the edge of the door and pulled it open. We stepped inside and closed the door behind us quickly. I lowered the hood on my cloak and, as my eyes adjusted to the gloom, I saw we were at the bottom of a staircase that went up one floor. It was indeed an emergency exit. The interior of the stairwell was dimly lit and there was nothing of ornamentation or writing to be seen to give us a clue as to what building we had entered. A brief sound of commotion outside the door we entered spurred us up the stairs.

We entered the door at the top of the stairs much easier and entered a dark hallway that ended in a set of colorful hanging beads. We moved quickly through the beads and walked into an ornate, gilded room filled with pillows, beds, and all manner of furniture upon which to lie down and engage in the building's main form of business. The room was chock full of snoozing green-skinned, slightly reptilian looking Progorians. Before I could even gasp, I felt a blade pressed against my neck. I imagined a twin was resting against Tar's jugular as well.

"Make any sound and I'll kill you and gut you where you stand," an angelic voice hissed in my ear.

CHAPTER 3
DROP DEAD GORGEOUS

I couldn't even swallow in shock, thinking the pressure of the sharp edge against my skin would be enough pressure to penetrate my skin.

"If you understand, don't make a sound. If you don't understand, simply say so and I'll get the killing over with, slicing your necks so far open you'll never make a sound again."

We remained obedient and silent. One of the Progorians mumbled something in their sleep and I felt an ever so slight increase in the pressure of the blade against my very blade vulnerable skin. The mumbling stopped and he resumed snoring. I felt sweat trickle down my throat and disappear from my skin at the blade's edge.

"Move slowly forward, watching your step," the voice continued whispering in my ear. If it hadn't been for the presence of the weapon under my chin, I would've sworn it was the most seductive voice I'd ever heard. My mind was otherwise occupied with walking forward gingerly, avoiding the random Progorian limb splayed into the walkway.

We moved forward until we entered another hallway. It was perhaps the most dangerous thirty meters I'd ever experienced. As we passed the threshold of the room, a barely audible hiss sounded behind us and the blade disappeared from my neck.

"You may speak quietly now but don't bother turning around. If you know who I am, you must also know I can kill you literally in the blink of an eye."

"Of course, Madame," I replied.

"Madame? You know who she is?" Tar asked. I could sense her shaking her head behind us.

"There's a staircase to your left. Walk to it slowly. Any sudden moves will result in a deadly bloodletting."

"Elle deVere, owner of the Courtesan Academy and sister of the head of the assassins' guild," I said as I walked carefully to the staircase. I felt the briefest prick of a blade putting a microscopic hole in the skin of my lower back.

"Half-sister. Gets your facts straight," the sultry voice purred. We reached the staircase and began to climb it.

"Duly noted," I responded. "Being so close to that part of the family business, she has all the skills required to deal with unruly patrons with deadly force if necessary."

"And while you two are most unruly, you're definitely not patrons."

"Well, hey since we're here-" Tar fell silent before he could finish his sentence. I suspected he felt the same kind of blade prick in his lower back.

"Doubtful you will ever be a patron here, Tar Reztap. I know exactly how many credits you're worth.

You don't pass the pre-qualifications to enter the front door."

"Hey! Okay, sorry." Tar's quick turn-around at being insulted informed me he probably had a second pinprick in his back, or possibly somewhere else.

We climbed up several floors in silence. As I walked, I noted the rich dark wood and velvety red walls with gold accents and designs. Decorative statues of marble and ornate, expensive paintings lined the walls. The impeccable carpeted stairs looked brand new, riveted into place by shiny gold brads. Great care was taken to keep the place looking rich and deserving of the most well-enriched clients.

"Beautiful place you have here," I said, wondering if I'd feel another stab in my back in return for my attempt at small talk.

"Upkeep would be a real pain without the regenerative surfaces throughout. It's still expensive, but none of this is actually the material it appears to be," Madame deVere said. I thought she almost sounded relieved to be able to talk to someone she wasn't trying to impress and imaginatively lie to. Of course, I hoped she wasn't unconcerned about our intimate knowledge of the surroundings because she was taking us to our certain death. Small talk could be the death of me.

"Go through the double doors ahead," she said as we reached the top of the stairs five floors up. We walked through the doors and entered a lovely sitting room unlike the rest of the building. The sunlit room had soft pastel colors on the fabric and walls, giving the room an uplifting appearance. It was tranquil.

Locks sounded on the double doors and our host let out a sigh.

"Okay, geniuses, whatever possessed you to think

you could escape military bounty hunters by coming in here?"

I took the chance to turn around. Madame deVere was strikingly attractive with pale violet hair and dressed in a black leather corset with a red lace-lined bodice. Her body was beautiful, toned, and undeniably deadly like a mesmerizing snake ready to strike.

"Dumb luck?" I said.

"That is something I hear the crew of the Bloated Namreg has plenty of. Are your cargo bays overflowing with it or something?"

"We didn't even realize it was your building," Tar said. He turned around as well and raised his eyebrows. He never concealed his lustful stares well.

"Don't get too comfortable, boys. I'm still deciding what to do with you," she said as she waved her knives at us and pointed to the left behind us. "Into the sun room."

We looked to where she was pointing and saw a small bay window area pushing out the side of the building. Walking into it, I looked out and saw a great view of a large portion of Selatarn. I estimated we were about six stories up. Down below, milling about the streets were a half dozen bounty hunters.

"The military, bounty hunters, and assassins have an agreement with me. I don't provide refuge to anyone they're after, and they don't come inside my place of business."

"Oh," I said.

"What?" Tar replied.

"Goodbye boys," Madame deVere said and the bottom dropped out from under us. We fell one floor until we hit the first of several well placed awnings slowing our fall. The process was anything but comfortable. It felt like falling through a solid wall. I imagined they were constructed of the same regenerative material as the ornate building interiors. As we fell thru the fifth one, our downward progress slowed to less than lethal speeds and it occurred to me we should have just given up in the bar. A carefully constructed mound of grass and fiber cushioned our landing on the surface of the asteroid and we painfully tumbled a few meters into the center of a large courtyard, surrounded by an assemblage of goggled bounty hunters, the leader of which gestured to a small building doorway with the same weapon we saw in Galloper's.

Considering the lethality of the laser cannon, we complied and went along with the ominous figure. This seemed to be the best plan of action until we reached a large, dark room and were clouted on the back of our heads, basically ensuring that it just wasn't going to be a nice day.

CHAPTER 4
CELLULAR DEGENERATES

When will I learn? How could I be so stupid?" Tar paced the cell and ran his fingers through his hair. Waking up on a military cruiser had darkened his mood considerably.

I watched my lifelong friend in silence. We met at a mining outpost in Alpha Centauri's giant asteroid belt. Tar had been mining to earn money for the docking permit at Selatarn. I had been visiting the mining outpost with my parents. At the time Tar mumbled something about missing a date just so he could pound on rocks all day. This intrigued me, not because I had never pounded on rocks before, but because I found it strange a kid our age would worry about dating a yucky girl. The subsequent chase through a series of mining tunnels to save her only to see him get rebuffed by her at the end confirmed my youthful suspicions not to mess with girls at all. We'd developed an inseparable friendship in the years since.

"Every time I walk into Galloper's something bad

happens to me. You'd think after the first twenty-two times I'd get a hint," Tar sat down on one of the bunks and stared at the bare steel walls of the cell. "What have I done to deserve such treatment?" He paused in thought. "Scratch that, what have they found out that I've done?"

We were soon joined by our captor, Rennifej Bartlett. As he entered, he deftly maneuvered his generous bulk around us. The dim light in the brig dully reflected off the shiny gold braid on the black velvet uniform. His jet black hair, graying at the temples, formed a receding hairline that neatly bordered the porcine face that had haunted many of Tar's worst nightmares.

He was a nefarious prankster who had recruited us for numerous escapades before, whether we liked it or not, and had obviously done so again. He gave, or rather, forced, all the thankless jobs on Tar. Knowing their family dynamic, I figured there had to be many a sordid tale in their upbringing that brought them to this mutual state of barely contained hate.

Rennifej had brought along a bodyguard to deter any hostilities from Tar. The bodyguard was a Neanderthal, a race of very strong, negligibly intelligent beings, who resembled prehistoric humans from my home planet, Terra. They were large and formidable enough that even I gave them a wide berth. Nobody in their right mind messed with a Neanderthal.

Just the same, I kept my eye on Tar. Rennifej brought out Tar's insane, foolish, and downright ornery side.

"So, Renni, how's it hangin'?" Tar chirped in a sarcastic, yet conversational tone. I sighed. This couldn't end well.

"Please refrain from such vulgar salutations. I'm not here to exchange pleasantries. I'm here to talk business."

"Talk away, gutter breath." Tar sported an insane smile.

"Right." Rennifej glared at Tar, then cleared his throat and continued. "You're going on a mission to save Princess Slurk from the evil clutches of Dyno Oynas."

"Do I have any say in this, sticky britches?" Tar spoke with a gleam in his eye. Tar told me years ago the only pleasant aspect of talking to Rennifej was insulting him with every breath.

"Yeoman, talk to him."

The large Neanderthal stepped over to Tar, let out a snort of disgust, and then bounced Tar's face off the Neanderthal's skull. This brief action did nothing to the Neanderthal but had an extremely detrimental effect on Tar's face.

Tar managed an unintelligible whisper.

"Thank you for the apology, Reztap. Your mission—go to the Drynta star system and retrieve Princess Slurk from Dyno's fortress on Alaga One's moon. That's not Alaga Two or Alaga Three, but Alaga One!"

"You're still upset about that little mix-up on Progor Three, aren't you?" Tar replied slowly and somewhat more politely. He gently massaged the impact zone on his face.

"That was Progor Two and it wasn't a little mix-up. You single-handedly started an intergalactic war five years ago between the Progorians and the Clachés which they're still fighting!" Rennifej paused to regain his composure, and then continued in a calm, but firm voice. "I would very much like to see you dead, Reztap.

Unfortunately, I've missed you every time I've shot at you."

A smug smile crept across Tar's face.

"Wish I could say the same, Renni. How is that left buttock, by the way? Can you sit down yet?" Tar chuckled.

"This conversation has ended, Reztap." Rennifej gave him an icy glare and turned to go. "You'll be free to go in a few hours. The details of your mission will be sent to your ship in transit."

Rennifej departed, leaving his Neanderthal companion behind. Tar smiled at the muscular humanoid. The smile conveyed a foolish bravado I recognized and dreaded.

"Please, no more talky-talky. Some things are better left unsaid," Tar cooed at the giant.

The yeoman grunted and turned to leave. Tar dropped a last goodbye.

"So long, salami-lips."

To my recollection, I don't think Tar's mouth had ever encountered so much knuckle hair.

CHAPTER 5
NEANDERTHALS AND ANDROIDS

After picking Tar up off the floor, I wondered why Tar didn't take his own advice and leave some things unsaid. Rennifej let us go a few minutes later. Making us wait had lost its appeal once Tar was rendered unconscious. I lugged my friend out of the military cruiser onto the space dock. Knowing he would wake up in a bad mood, I mentally reviewed all of the available remedies for that aggrieved state of mind. A special brew that always helped me rose to the top of the list.

Several hours later, Tar woke up in a generally bad mood. He hit the intercom, rousing me from my ministrations on behalf of our new mission.

"Did you dump all of the dirty laundry into my cabin?" Tar asked.

"Wimp," I replied. I figured he was referring to the gift I'd left him since I'd removed his dirty laundry earlier with the help of biohazard gloves and a gas mask.

"Oh, seriously?" I guessed Tar had spotted the cup sitting on the table with steam floating out of it; Neanderthals just weren't his cup of tea. As I was a heartier trader then he, I really enjoyed Neanderthal tea. Tar preferred to stay away from Neanderthals altogether.

The concept of Neanderthal tea was formerly thought to be absurd, until recent developments in quality brewing techniques allowed the Neanderthal to survive the brewing process. This created a much needed job market for Neanderthals, who previously could only hold jobs involving terrorizing locals, being yeomen on military vessels, and elephant wrestling. Now this large, hairy race could be brewed for approximately ten cups a week, take a week off to get their stench and dirt ratio back up to proper brewing levels, and get brewed once again. It paid very well and left a lot of free time for engaging in their favorite sport of elephant wrestling; it was their favorite because they seemed to be the only race that could safely participate in the sport.

To my surprise, Tar appeared on the bridge dressed in a new jumpsuit quicker than stink can accumulate on a Neanderthal. I pondered why I continued cleaning Tar's jumpsuits while he sniffed the curious lemon fresh scent of his garment.

The voice screaming from the speakers jolted us both out of our reverie.

"You flaming maladroit!" The phrase echoed throughout the bridge.

"Incompetent, bumbling idiot!" The words emerged flawlessly from the speakers hidden behind the walls of the bridge.

I pointed at a display which showed a strange series of calculations streaming across it.

"The ghost," I whispered.

The numbers involved a little used voice reproduction program in one of the main computers data banks. The ghost ran through the parameters of the voice reproduction program, raised the volume of the target word "idiot" 0.09 decibels and toggled the pitch. It ran the phrase through the speaker system one more time.

"Incompetent, bumbling idiot!"

The program indicated success and closed down.

"That has got to be Renni infiltrating the system," Tar said.

"I'll see what I can do to track down our wayward digital intruder."

I set to work and traced every wire and communication link, finding a few surprises in the search but nothing leading directly to our ghost. There was a central communication backbone and two redundant backbones leading from the bridge to the rest of the ship; there was no way to trace these physically without tearing the ship apart. I even double checked the quantum light accelerators for any anomalies, but found them problem free. While I delved deep into the communication relays, transmitters, receivers and signal boosters, Tar attended to the automated controls preparing the shuttle for our incursion to Alaga One's sole satellite.

I removed myself from the guts of the communications console when I heard Tar whistling happily. After spending so much time unconscious, I doubted he could be in a good mood. It set me on edge.

"Tar?"

Tar smiled as he took in the entire bridge lit up. Monitors showed the surrounding space dock and panels with various indicator dials, lights, and alarms functioned perfectly.

"This ship really warms my heart, Gorth. She may not look like much on the outside, but she's beautiful in here."

"And good morning to you too. You appear to be in an unusually good mood after nine hours waiting for your brain to stop swelling. Was it the Neanderthal tea?"

Tar didn't even make a face at the mention of the repulsive beverage.

"Nope." He sucked in a breath of recycled air. "It was the Gadrazoon that did it."

"Gadrazoon! Where?!" I screamed, anxious for a once in a decade chance at pure sensual delight. Gadrazoons were known across the universe for mating only one week every ten years. But when they did mate, did they ever mate!

"Just thinking about one, that's all. I pulled out a bottle of Lobotomy Slammer and thought about how bad I'd feel after drinking it. Of course, only sex with a Gadrazoon would bring me out of it."

"Great, now you've got me depressed."

That Tar had a bottle of Lobotomy Slammer, the strongest liquor available, didn't surprise me. However, casually throwing out the possible, no matter how unlikely, presence of a Gadrazoon was unforgivable. I flicked a few switches, checked the readout on the monitor in front of me, and smiled grimly. For a Gadrazoon, I would consider delaying our departure. As it was, I had to give Tar the bad news.

"Of course, I'm sure you'll join me in my

depression soon enough. We have to pull out our back-up navigator."

Tar almost swallowed his tongue in shock.

"Wait a minute, what happened to the one Tob located for us?"

"You put him out of commission," I answered with as straight a face as I could muster. I thought I might as well enjoy this while I could.

"What do you mean I 'put him out of commission'? I haven't even seen him yet!"

"No?" I raised my eyebrows into two perfect arches. "Who do you think you hit on the head the minute we walked into Galloper's?"

"That kid?"

"Yeah, that kid. He was possibly the only navigator on Selatarn who hadn't been briefed on the dangers of serving on board our ship. As wild as the odds are, he'd never heard of you before meeting Tob, who filled his head with tales of action and adventure. I instructed Tob not to let the kid talk to anyone informed until we get back. Meanwhile, since you're responsible for our current predicament, you get to pull out Chuck."

I watched in amusement as a shudder of horror rattled Tar's spine. His stomach threatened to perform a nasty upheaval. A nervous twitch danced under his left eyebrow.

"Gorth, please, I'll do anything, and I do mean anything, to avoid letting Chuck out again!" His voice quivered in sincere desperation. "Let's wait until the kid's better, okay?"

"Think Rennifej will wait that long? He might send the yeoman over to talk to you again."

I was slightly sympathetic. I really felt sorry for Tar because of the horror that he was about to unleash on himself. But it was a horror of his own making, so I didn't feel too sorry for him.

"Salami-lips?" Tar winced. "Right. Chuck it is then."

Tar walked to the rear of the bridge. He paused at the compartment before him. "Gorth, you realize this is the third worst thing I've ever encountered in my life. It ranks just below taxes and women's lib."

"That does not surprise me in the slightest." On the steel door before Tar, written in bold red letters on a yellow background, was a message that read:

IF YOU OPEN THIS DOOR, YOUR GUTS WILL BE SUCKED OUT OF YOU THROUGH YOUR NOSE, YOU'LL BE INSTANTANEOUSLY CASTRATED BY A WILD MAN WITH NEEDLE NOSE PLIERS, YOUR EYEBALLS WILL BE COOKED TO A TENDER, GOLDEN BROWN WHILE THEY ARE STILL OCCUPYING YOUR THEN MEDIUM RARE EYESOCKETS, OR SOMETHING EVEN WORSE COULD HAPPEN TO YOU... THINK ABOUT IT!!!

Tar shut his eyes. "Goodbye, cruel world," he said as he pushed the button marked 'DANGER' on the panel next to the door and it slid open with an ominous whoosh.

Tar swallowed hard before opening his eyes. Inside the compartment, a blonde male android stood motionless, dressed in a shocking pink jumpsuit trimmed with fluorescent yellow material. Tar shuddered and raised his eyes to the ceiling. Grimacing, he reached over and flicked a switch on the side of the android's abdomen.

"Oooh, Captain," the android cooed in a high male voice. "You turn me on."

"Don't I always?" Tar replied glumly, to which the android only giggled. "Come on, Chuck, let's get this over with."

"Oh Rezzy, I just love how you take control of the situation." Chuck cuddled up to Tar, who was obviously repulsed by the android's carrying on. Tar kept a civil tongue. We both knew that if he upset Chuck, the flamboyant automaton would just sit and pout instead of doing his work.

"Okay, Chuck, it's time to put your talents to work."

A look of glee broke out on the android's face. Chuck reached behind Tar and pinched him.

"It's about time, Rezzy!"

Tar shuffled away from Chuck. I imagine he was torn between repulsion and the impulse to strangle Chuck.

"I mean set a course for Alaga... uh... um..." Tar ordered in a controlled voice, hiding his anger and embarrassment.

"Alaga One, Chuck," I said, eager to avoid starting another intergalactic war. I immersed myself in the innards of the combat control console and resumed my search for the ghost.

"Well, that's no fun," Chuck said as he walked to the navigation console.

While Chuck plotted our course to Alaga One, Tar crawled under the console. "Your brother is evil, setting that thing on us!" Tar whispered.

"I told you not to insult Natin, but you went right ahead and did it, didn't you?"

"Natin's a-" Tar stopped himself and took a breath, selecting a different word. "An idiot!"

"Well, he's a smart idiot, smart enough to reprogram Chuck in a greatly exaggerated image of himself. Besides, he didn't set it on us, he set it on you," I smiled, exultant in my superior position in the conversation.

"That flutterby is going to pay for this, mark my words!"

"All you have to do is apologize, Tar."

"Never!" Tar hissed. "I'd rather die!"

"Oh, Rezzy," came an all too familiar voice, making Tar grimace. "I'm done. Want to play doctor now?"

"Prepare to die, Tar," I said as I tugged at a cable that didn't look familiar.

Tar just sneered at me.

"Chuck," Tar said, thinking quicker than I've seen him do in a long time. "I was just thinking of how much you'd like to redecorate the galley."

CHAPTER 6
BATTLE OF TWITS

U p and at 'em, Tar."

"Go kiss a…" mumbled Tar as he struggled to consciousness. He opened his eyes and screamed. "Senuvian Drot!"

I dangled a jumbled mass of conduit wires directly above Tar's head, realizing for a split second Tar would think a Senuvian Drot was attacking him.

Senuvian Drots were vicious cyborg jellyfish that would suck off your face in two seconds flat. They were sold for a hefty profit to an illegally working group of cosmetic surgeons who were well known for giving their customers new faces.

"Knew that would wake you up," I chuckled as Tar shoved the jumbled mass away from his face.

"Last time I saw anything like that was when that idiot android brought me a Drot he'd just killed; only he didn't tell me it was dead until after he set in on the console in front of me. I could've killed him." Tar held his head in his hands. Screaming first thing in the morning had definite disadvantages.

"Can't kill an android, you just turn them off." I bit into a multi-colored gorglemelon while frowning at a pile of dirty laundry on the floor of the cabin. I was certain it had just moved.

"Gods, can't you eat that somewhere else?" Tar pulled on a tan jumpsuit. "Makes me sick." He stepped out of the cabin.

"The man just can't appreciate good food," I said as I stepped through the doorway after Tar. I squeezed the fruit in my hand; it made a gorgle sound. I had a weakness for gorglemelons.

It was at this moment, that the following transpired, as revealed by logs I discovered later:

The computer filled up its spare time making endless calculations concerning the release of The Golden Sabre's sole passenger and owner from cryogenic hibernation. It calculated everything from his heartbeat and blood pressure to his projected actions when he discovered what year it wasn't. By the computer's reckoning, the passenger's ire would double every extra year he spent in suspended animation; at this point in time, 13.673 years overdue. From a meticulous interpretation of its calculations, the computer predicted the complete and total destruction of 4.269 civilizations by the foreseen rampaging of the ship's single living inhabitant. Of course, it had to estimate several factors in its calculations; however, the computer was certain that the person assigned to wake the sleeper would not be the one to do so. If a computer could wrinkle its nose, this computer most certainly would; it knew the caliber of the man now destined to awaken the sleeper.

The computer worked very hard for the last three weeks to correct the unforeseen errors in the scheme of things. While it was reasonably sure its slumbering master would be very disappointed with his savior, it had set up the best possible test for the lumbering clod of a hero, taking all the resources at hand and constructing this rescue scenario. When he awoke, the owner would be pleased with the computer's efforts, if not with the results of this test. Only time would tell what kind of man would unlock the cryogenic chamber.

Tar's mood visibly dampened the minute he stepped on the bridge. There, pink clad arms outstretched, was Chuck.

"Not now, Chuck, I've got a headache."

"You've always got a headache!" Chuck folded his arms in front of him.

Tar sighed.

Chuck was not an evil creation, regardless of what Tar continually stated. Chuck merely had a little reprogramming done to his personality subroutines by my younger brother, Natin. It had all started at a traders' convention held on Selatarn three years earlier. Tar purchased Chuck, a navigational android, to pilot the ship during battles. The tide usually went in our favor if the human crew manned the weapons. A navigational android also came in handy during the long stretches of interstellar space travel between solar systems which the living crew spent in suspended hibernation. At the moment of purchase, Chuck had a normal personality, nothing special, and certainly nothing homosexual—until Natin came onto the scene.

Tar met Natin before and had been less than polite at that first meeting. At the traders' convention, however, Tar acted overtly rude and callous. Tar had little tolerance for any lifestyle that varied too greatly from his own and Natin's lifestyle was a far cry from Tar's. Natin was a soft spoken man who never meant harm to anyone; his one fault, in Tar's eyes, was he was gay. Natin was used to a little ribbing for his choice in sexual partners, and he didn't mind as long as the joking didn't get out of hand. He withstood nearly an hour of Tar's nasty jokes and vicious barbs and then told Tar to knock it off. That really set Tar off and he got so nasty that he started to draw a crowd. I tried to calm him down, but he would have none of it. Natin couldn't get in a word edgewise while Tar went on about his 'weaknesses.' After a while, Natin didn't bother trying. He just formulated his revenge, listening intently to every word Tar said. With this blueprint from Tar's own lips, Natin reprogrammed Chuck into everything Tar described as a homosexual male, adding a few choice touches of his own. He left a message pinned to Chuck inside the Bloated Namreg, telling Tar that all he had to do to get Chuck's program reverted to the original baseline was apologize... in the public square on Selatarn, where Tar said all the offensive words in the first place.

Tar pleaded with me to get Natin to change Chuck back, but I supported my brother and refused. Tar even tried to get android programmers to reprogram Chuck, but no one would deal with him because he'd treated one of their fellow programmers so badly. The dealer who sold Chuck to Tar refused an exchange or refund because of his altered programming. Tar could suffer with Chuck's reprogramming or apologize to Natin. For the last three years, Tar chose to suffer the reprogramming; but even I wasn't sure how much more he could take.

I strolled onto the bridge sporting a brown bandana.

Tar took one look at me and pulled an identical bandana out of his jumpsuit and tied it around his own head. Chuck looked puzzled.

"What's with the bandanas, fellas?" Chuck said in his distinctive, flamboyant voice. Tar got a pained look on his face as he listened to Chuck talking.

Up until now, we'd had a human navigator pilot for the Namreg crew when the chance of battle was imminent. Chuck only came out of the closet for long hauls between solar systems, handling the piloting while Tar and I slept in cryogenic sleeping chambers. The unfortunate incident on Selatarn had thwarted our plans for a human taking that spot again. Our former live crew member had suffered a loss of appetite for adventure. It also may have been the loss of several limbs that led to his early retirement.

"Well," I said. "Whenever there's a possibility of the Namreg going into battle, the crew dons brown bandanas for good luck. Here's yours."

I pulled a brown bandana out of my pocket and gave it to Chuck. He handled it like it was a dead animal, dropping it to the ground a few seconds later.

"Oh no! Never! Brown clashes with my outfit."

"What doesn't?" Tar mumbled.

"I'm terribly sorry, but it's against my programming to dress unfashionably. I simply can't wear a brown bandana."

"So wear a pink one!" Tar said.

"I never thought of that," Chuck said as he produced a yellow polka-dotted, pink bandana from his back pocket and tied it around his head. I'd never seen anything quite like it before. Tar's face blanched.

"Well, how does it look?"

"Don't run for office," I said.

Tar grabbed his mouth and made a sound much

like the one he made after a long night of enjoying too much liquor and ran to the bathroom. When he returned, he gave his reply.

"Perfect, Chuck. Just perfect." Tar turned to me and whispered. "I smell impending disaster looming on the horizon."

Tar tightened a securing strap near the top of the bridge view screen and wrinkled his nose. He walked back to me and whispered. "Never mind. It was just my jumpsuit; remind me to change it before we reach Alaga One."

Several seconds later, Chuck nearly jumped out of his skin when the battle alarm blasted the bridge personnel with clear, dulcet tones. The room glowed with the red shimmer of the combat alert lights. Tar and I wasted no time getting into our gunner seats. Chuck walked with dainty steps to the navigator's seat and strapped in. We both observed him with a hint of concern; this was Chuck's first battle. He knew how to pilot the ship in battle. We just weren't sure whether or not he would do it.

"Okay, Chuck, you're piloting this baby. Let's blast 'em!"

"Right on, Rezzy!"

"By the way, who are we blasting?" Tar asked.

"It looks like the Insane Moth, a small battleship from Rimtiki Lumdung," I deduced from the readouts on the bridge's main screen. I knew my battleships pretty well.

"Yee-haw! Five hundred points for whoever lands the first blow!" Tar loved going into battle.

The Insane Moth was only slightly larger than the Bloated Namreg. No matter how small a battleship was, however, they were all powerful. The Insane Moth was no exception. This particular battleship had an unusual structural design; I mused at how it resembled a Terran fruit called a banana. A large power reserve globe rested on the center of the ship, making it appear as if the globe caused the ship to bow in the middle. Although it looked comical, the ship was extremely deadly. The Rimtikians were a volatile lot opting to shoot first and not ever bother asking questions.

The Namreg's titungsteel superstructure, comprised of a titanium and tungsten steel alloy, groaned under the strain of maneuvering in battle. We cruised by the port side of the Moth, fired, and missed. The Namreg's fore thrusters fired powerfully, shooting the nose of the Namreg directly up, clearly surprising the crew aboard the Moth who likely thought our less than graceful looking ship would not be very maneuverable. The Rimtikians return volley of missiles and laser fire flew far from striking their target.

The Namreg's automated defenses took care of anything that got too close for comfort. The Namreg had fewer guns, but those guns were deceptively powerful; if we got off a clean shot, the Moth's automated defenses wouldn't stand a chance of stopping it. As the Namreg started around for another run, the Moth got another chance to fire; this time much closer to their target. Chuck, surprisingly adept at stellar combat, brought the Namreg around with a fairly large asteroid passing directly between the Moth and the Namreg, timed just right for the entire second volley from the Moth and the asteroid to obliterate each other. Now the Moth was a sitting duck. Tar smiled as he squeezed the trigger. Suddenly, the Namreg lurched violently; the thrusters going haywire.

"Oh no!" came a scream from the navigator's

console. The Namreg was on a collision course with the Moth.

"What's wrong?" Tar shouted from the left gunner's seat.

"I broke a nail!"

We turned around and looked at the navigator's station just in time to see Chuck heading away from the navigation console toward the bridge entrance.

"What are you doing?!" Tar screamed, though it came out as more of a rasp as he pulled at the belt restraints anchoring him in the seat.

"I've got to go fix it," Chuck said as he walked off the bridge, leaving the navigation controls on automatic causing the ship to lock on its present collision course with the Moth.

"CHUCK!"

When he got no reply, Tar quickly unstrapped himself, jumped out of the gunner's seat, and landed running. The Namreg shuddered as the ship's automated defenses struggled to keep it untouched by enemy fire. The delay gave the Moth time to fire another volley and the Namreg was an easy target with no one at the helm. The enemy easily struck us now that we no longer changed course; not a particularly proud accomplishment for the Rimtikians, but they probably wouldn't tell anybody they only started hitting an enemy ship when it stopped maneuvering.

"You'll have to pull out the back-up," Tar said from the navigator's seat, throwing switches to stabilize the shaking ship. "I put up with insufferable indignities just so our back-up can do his nails in the heat of battle. Beautiful!" Tar pushed a couple of buttons and the ship stopped shuddering.

"Nobody's perfect," I said. Now that the ship stopped shaking, I could draw an accurate bead on my target. I aimed for the power globe atop the center of the Moth and fired; the powerful pulse laser cannon glowed brightly from the port side of the Namreg. The Moth's automated defenses struggled to diffuse the condensed beam of light headed for its power storage unit. At the same time, they fired off another volley at the Namreg. The universe at large was well aware of the concept of mutually assured destruction.

The powerful beam from the pulse laser cannon tore into the globe, boring a huge hole through its center. The Moth shuddered as all of its pressurized cabins ruptured from the sudden power flux. The Moth's last volley hadn't been in vain, however; a single missile found its way through the Namreg's defenses and impacted on the port side. There was a small hole in the side of the Namreg, but the damage appeared minimal.

"Well, that wasn't so..." Tar's face froze with a half-smile. The controls refused to respond to his commands. The Namreg remained on a collision course with the Moth.

Tar wiped his brow, yanked open a panel in front of him and grabbed hold of the Namreg's emergency directional thruster control stick. He activated the thrusters and the ship lurched. I screamed.

"A little easy on those curves, please! I had a big breakfast and I don't fancy seeing it all over my lap!"

Tar ignored my pleas of mercy and pulled on the stick with all his might. It snapped.

"Darn."

Although it was no longer on a head-on collision course, the Namreg was, nevertheless, going to hit the Moth. The ship stopped shuddering as it glided towards the Moth. I realized what had happened the minute the ship stopped vibrating. As we always did in crisis situations aboard the Namreg, Tar and I looked at the ceiling and we recited a prayer in unison.

"Please God, don't trash my genitals."

The far port side of the Namreg collided with the bridge of the Moth. Both ships shuddered while the damage was being done.

"Watch over my mother and father."

The wrenching sound of the collision echoed throughout the ship.

"Let the Enigmas win a game for once."

Smoke billowed from the corridor leading onto the bridge.

"Thanks, God. Keep in touch." We bowed our heads as we finished our prayer.

Chuck came running onto the bridge, and as the artificial gravity ceased to function, went flying through the air.

"Oh God! Don't let me die!" Chuck screamed.

"God," Tar said calmly. "Please... kill Chuck."

Tar shook his head in despair as Chuck bounced off a wall and giggled.

"This is kind of fun!" Chuck said as he floated over Tar's head.

The Bloated Namreg and Insane Moth floated away from each other. The Moth was in infinitely worse shape than the Namreg. It no longer possessed a single intact compartment from our vantage point. Debris surrounded the wreckage in all directions, and it floated away from the collision, powerless. Every few seconds a crackle of energy residue rippled along its exterior radiating from the punctured energy globe, but other than that, nothing moved.

The Namreg, on the other hand, had all functions at least partially operational except, due to Tar's mismanagement, the entire navigational system. A large chunk of the port side of the ship had disappeared. Our ship floated away from the impact, slowly spinning on its axis like a small yellow moon.

We surveyed the damage report scrolling up on the screen, the computer rating all damage on a scale of one to ten: one being slightly scratched, ten being completely missing. The galley, which Chuck had spent the last week redecorating, had a ten next to it. An evil grin crept across Tar's face. He loved to torment Chuck. He flipped a switch and returned artificial gravity to the ship. Chuck dropped to the deck with a muffled, metallic thud.

"Oh no. Chuck, I'm so sorry."

I glanced over at Tar, who spoke the words with a smile on his face.

Chuck gave Tar a blank stare. Tar rarely spoke politely to him.

"About what, Rezzy darling?"

"The galley."

"What about the galley?" Chuck still retained an innocent naïveté about deception and being tormented, evident in his polite voicing of the question.

"I'm afraid it's... gone."

"What?" Chuck quickly lost his naïveté, paused momentarily for a quick dose of shock, and then broke down into uncontrollable sobbing. "Oh, Rezzy... I'm sorry. I didn't mean for this to happen," Chuck choked out between sobs.

"Chuck, I expect you to start rebuilding it as soon as we get back into port."

Chuck stopped sobbing.

"What do you care about the galley for?" Chuck asked between sniffles.

Tar frowned and looked around the bridge for a

moment. "Isn't that what you were upset about?"

A look of disbelief broke out on Chuck's face.

"The galley decorations. You remember the centerpiece?"

"Well." Tar squirmed in his seat. I was a bit concerned about Tar lying under the scrutinizing gaze of a possibly emotionally unstable android. They were quite strong, and we'd never encountered Chuck when he was angry.

"Sure, I stopped by and glanced around briefly before I came up to the bridge."

"And you didn't see the scarf?"

I watched in amazement as goose bumps suddenly appeared in great number on Tar's arms.

"Scarf?" Tar choked the word out of his suddenly constricted airway.

"Yes, your red scarf. I hung it up around the outer port hole, sort of like a wreath; it was tied in a very ornamental knot at the bottom. It contrasted wonderfully with the chartreuse color of the wall."

"Red... scarf..."

"Yes. Oh Rezzy, I wish you could have seen it. There was a dancing hologram of your mother emanating from that scarf. It was so beautiful. For a woman, your mother really is fairly decent looking."

"Mom's... red... scarf..." The color of Tar's face grew red and the veins on his neck thickened into red hoses. His eyes jerked wildly.

"Yes," Chuck continued oblivious to Tar's facial contortions. He walked up next to Tar. "I arranged all the tables so they were concentric around the scarf and—" Chuck stopped moving, a look of surprise frozen on his face. Tar had just turned him off.

Struggling with the straps of the navigational chair, Tar called out to me. "Gorth! We've got to go back!"

On the far side of the bridge, I attempted a manual adjustment of the thruster circuits to stop the ship's spinning.

"Huh?" I pulled my arm out from inside a control panel. Several wires dangled from my jumpsuit.

"We gotta turn around now!"

"Look, Tar. I don't have time for jokes right now. If we don't get navigational control back pretty soon, we may have a nasty rendezvous with a wayward asteroid. Primary controls ran along the port side and got severed by the collision. You managed to short-circuit the backup navigation. So, give the comedy routine a rest." I stuck my head under the console.

Tar finally got free of the navigator seat's straps and stumbled to me. He grabbed my jumpsuit lapel and dragged me out from under the control panel. I looked at him like he was crazy. Seeing the look on Tar's face, I was certain he had lost it.

"Gorth," Tar squeaked, gasping for air. "That idiot android put my mom's red scarf in the galley...now it's back there with the Insane Moth..." Tar looked like he was going to collapse.

Tar's family dynamic was a special, sordid deal that bore some explanation, at least as far as I understood it. Tar's mother was Antillikus Madriana Rejentcia Tallusiaka Bartlett Reztap, First Premier of Andros, second in command to the great Emperor of Andros, Duchess of Laxton, and High Priestess of the Valoran Clan of the Stick. She preferred to be called Anty. It was around Anty, the social and political black hole of Andros, that the rest of the family orbited. Some of them spun wildly out of control. Antillikus was her given name, the rest were the surnames of her various husbands, Tar's father being the last in the line. It sounded fancy, but in reality, that made Tar the last and youngest of his twenty-three siblings, albeit the only son of his father.

It was into this brood Tar was born and had to fight for survival, recognition and, best of all, clothing. His toughness and tenacity were born of this upbringing and from the Reztap lineage which had some respectability thirty years ago when his mother and father were first wed. That respectability had long since faded into history. Tar was forced to make his own way in the world unknown and, as he mentioned time and again, unappreciated.

I set my buddy down on the deck of the bridge and rested his head against the bulkhead. I knew the story of the scarf. I also knew that Tar was in a whole heap of trouble. Unfortunately, we couldn't do a thing about it at the moment. The ship had to be put back under our control or in short order we wouldn't be worrying about anything. Our present course still led us in the direction we needed to go, but a stray asteroid could stop us dead in space at any moment. I resumed my efforts on the thruster circuits.

Tar stared silently as stars spun by on the main viewer. Rumor was that Dyno Oynas would be moving the Princess within the month. We both knew we couldn't afford to go back for the scarf anyway.

"Piss water," he mumbled as his head cleared.

"Mom's gonna kill me..."

CHAPTER 7
SLUDGE HAPPENS

Three days after the incident with the Insane Moth, the Bloated Namreg established orbit around the second moon of Alaga Two. Chuck still stood motionless next to the navigator's console. Tar hadn't quite forgiven Chuck for the disaster with the red scarf; Anty would be angry with the loss of her gift and even intergalactic distances wouldn't insulate Tar from her wrath. However, now that we could go no further in the Namreg, it was necessary to 'revive' Chuck so Tar and I could continue the trip to Alaga One's moon in the ship's short range shuttle, The Juniper Pod.

"I don't see why we can't just leave it unmanned except for our android statue here," Tar said.

"No."

"No one's ever broken in."

"Look," I said. "We have enough bad things happen that I don't want to encourage a preventable disaster. Can we just leave it at that?"

Tar stared at the floor a moment. He nodded. "Okay, you can."

"No." I cut him off before he could shirk the responsibility. "You have to turn him back on so he believes you have confidence in him. If I do it, it will nag at him and we could come back to a frazzled and unstable android who could quite frankly do any number of things to this ship in our absence."

Tar sighed and walked over to Chuck. Tar was a bit lazy about cleaning out the ship's ventilation system, so a thin layer of dust had accumulated on Chuck's skin and clothing. Tar reached down and flipped the switch that would bring Chuck back to 'consciousness.'

"Gosh, Rez."

"Don't even think about speaking in my presence, Chuck." Tar cut the android off before he could say much. "I haven't even come close to forgiving you for... I can't even take the time to list all the things you've done this time. Just keep silent. Do not speak unless spoken too. Do you understand?" Tar glared at Chuck, who quivered.

"Yes, Rezzy."

"Good, now go dust yourself. Gorth and I will be leaving in The Juniper Pod in a little under half an hour, so hurry."

Chuck left the bridge without saying a word. I watched the transaction between Tar and the android and shook my head.

"Don't you think you were a little hard on him?"

Tar's jaw dropped open, his eyes got wide and he threw his hands up in the air.

"Gorth, he's just a machine!"

"So." I stood up and paced the length of the bridge. "That means that you've been angry with a machine for three days now. Right?"

"Not exactly." Tar rolled his eyes.

"Well, you didn't get upset with the control stick when it broke in the middle of battle. And you didn't get upset with the directional thrusters for failing to operate after they'd been damaged by the Insane Moth's last shot."

"What are you getting at Gorth?"

"Chuck is just obeying his programming, which you don't have the guts to get changed. So I'm telling you all the things which Chuck has done wrong are basically your fault. You haven't been angry with him for the last three days. You've been angry with yourself."

"Geez, can't I get angry without being psychoanalyzed?" Tar shook his head. "Why do you have to find problems where there weren't any before?"

"Tar, do you realize you are truly hopeless?"

"Yes. It's the one factor in my personality that will never change. I've worked hard to get where I'm not at today."

I glared at Tar.

Tar raised his hands in surrender. "Okay, okay. I'll let Chuck off the hook."

A few minutes later, Chuck walked in. There wasn't a speck of dust on him. His head hung as he walked to the navigation console.

"Chuck."

Chuck raised his head, revealing his pouty lips and mournful eyes.

"Yes, Rezzy."

"You can stop moping. I'm not mad at you anymore."

A smile lit up Chuck's face and then he frowned.

"Why aren't you mad at me anymore, dearest?"

"Because." Tar tried not to let the word 'dearest' nettle him. "Gorth won't let me enjoy a good temper tantrum." Tar smiled in my direction. I just raised my eyes to the ceiling.

"But that does not mean I won't... do something terrible to you if you ever leave your post again in the middle of a battle. Understand?"

"Yes, darling."

Tar closed his eyes and took a deep breath. "Go clean out the ventilation filters, Chuck."

Tar and I were fully geared up when we climbed into The Juniper Pod thirty minutes later. The interior of the shuttle bay matched the yellow glow of the Namreg's exterior. The Juniper Pod's dull gray exterior facilitated a simple camouflage technique for hiding in plain sight on dull gray soil. The Namreg had several different colored shuttles, but we used The Juniper Pod most often.

"If that android wrecks the Namreg, I'll dismantle the son-of a-"

"Ah, ah," I interrupted. "No vulgarity while I'm the pilot."

"-microchip," Tar finished. "Too many darlings and dearests for me to stomach."

I mused he might get so angry he would actually contemplate apologizing to Natin.

The engines of The Juniper Pod whined to ready status. After checking the shuttle's air locks and hull integrity, I activated the shuttle bay departure sequence. The sound of the engines died away as the air in the pressurized shuttle bay filtered out into storage tanks hidden behind the walls. Soon, the atmosphere inside the shuttle bay mirrored the cold vacuum of space, and the shuttle bay doors opened.

The dull gray shuttle floated silently out of the shuttle bay. With a delicate touch, I maneuvered the small ship on directional thrusters only. When we reached a safe distance from the Namreg, I opened the throttle on the main engines and we streaked away from the big yellow ship.

At a later point and time, in my attempt to remedy a small mistake on my part, I dug through the files in our video surveillance system and pulled up the ones time-stamped for the moments directly after we left the Namreg. I recovered the following activity:

Inside the Namreg, Chuck watched The Juniper Pod fade away into the blackness of space.

"They always leave me behind," he mumbled. "I never get to have any fun..."

Chuck got up and walked over to an unmarked panel near the back of the bridge. He pressed his hand against the panel; it slid open with a faint hiss. Chuck reached inside and pulled out a holovideo chit entitled 'Men in Drag.'

"But, I can always improvise," Chuck giggled, walking off the bridge with chit in hand.

When the orbiting visage of the Namreg disappeared behind us, I let out a deep, dark chuckle and rubbed my hands together. Tar turned and looked at me with raised eyebrows.

"Something funny?" Tar asked.

"Oh, you might say that."

"Uh, care to let your good ol' buddy in on it?"

"Well," I replied, still chuckling. "I was hoping to save this for when we were done, but I'm just busting to tell you."

I paused for about thirty seconds and I remained

silent with a smile on my face. Tar couldn't stand the suspense.

"TELL ME, ALREADY!"

"Well," I began chuckling again, "when I sorted out all of those circuits after we had our battle with the Insane Moth, I accidentally found Chuck's secret hiding place. I connected what should have been the overload warning light for the left lower aft main thruster and one of the panels near the back of the bridge slid open. Inside it, I found this holovideo homosexual male pornography chit. To make a long story short, I switched labels with one of our holovideo heterosexual female pornography chits. The way I figure it, he should be viewing it right about... now!"

On the audio recording from various portions of the Namreg, I recovered a perfectly timed solitary, blood curdling scream echoing throughout the empty corridors of the ship.

"Gorth, my friend," Tar said smiling. "You are the best friend anyone could ask for, thanks."

"Don't mention it."

"I was concerned you had gone insane and, piloting us at ridiculous speeds through an asteroid belt, would ram us into an uncaring hunk of rock. I'm glad to see I was wrong."

An upsetting thought struck Tar. His smile lost some of its enthusiasm.

"Gorth, when you switched the chits, do you mean Chuck's chit is now under a false name in our collection?"

"That's right."

"I don't suppose you could tell me off hand which of our chits you switched with Chuck's could you?"

There was a brief period of silence. "Say 'yes,' Gorth." Tar lost his smile. I looked at Tar, shrugged my shoulders and said, "Oops."

Alaga One's orbital companion loomed in the central view port of the shuttle. The small moon matched the same dull gray color of the shuttle; the surface pitted with dozens of craters from the collisions of fairly large meteorites. I maneuvered the shuttle under the detection screen and into one of the larger craters. The fortress defenses weren't calibrated to detect anything that wouldn't be considered a menace. The Juniper Pod's small radar signature ensured it wouldn't be considered a serious threat to the forces inside and around the fortress.

On board the shuttle, we experienced an uneasy truce of silence as we glided in for a landing, sending up a small flurry of particulate lunar matter as the landing thrusters kicked on. A small 'thud' sounded as we settled onto the shifting dust. A whoosh of escaping air pressure broke the silence as the hatch to The Juniper Pod folded out into a ramp. I emerged alone from the shuttle, dressed in an environment suit and walked slowly down the ramp, adjusting the density settings on my apparel to accommodate the lighter gravity. When I stepped off the bottom of the ramp, Tar came out of the shuttle also dressed in his environment suit. Tar clunked down the ramp; stomping his weighted boots with each step.

"Oops?" Tar intoned over the headset.

"Tar, give me a break. I didn't purposely forget which chit I switched! It was a mistake anybody could make," I pleaded, waving my arms for no significant reason except to relieve my anxiety which it failed to do. Tar walked away from the shuttle, understandably miffed. As far as he was concerned, his entire collection of holovideo pornography chits had been rendered useless. The chance of running across Chuck's chit drowned out his desire to view any of them, the unfortunate side effect of advanced holographic technology "totally" immersing the viewer in the scene.

Tar looked left and right several times over the course of fifteen minutes. He shrugged his shoulders.

"I don't know where he is. He's supposed to be here. I told him 1500 hours, it's 1515 now, what do you want from me?" Tar tried to sound as innocent as he could.

I just glared at him. On top of the fact that I had to view all the chits when we got back to the Namreg, we'd been standing behind a large boulder for over half an hour doing absolutely nothing. All of this had soured my normally good mood. We were still a pretty fair distance from the fortress. This was where we were supposed to meet our contact who would get us inside undetected. I was bored, pissed and, worst of all, I knew this would happen. One of the main reasons I stayed with Tar included the adrenalin rushes from getting us out of the predicaments he always got us into. From climbing out of the escape pod wreckage on Progor Two to running from blood-crazed natives on Mallax's mud flats, narrow escapes peppered our missions with increasing frequency. At times like this, boot deep in the dust of a remote moon I most often wondered just to what extent my sanity would allow me to continue these actions.

"Why is it that anything you arrange winds up more screwed up than if we'd just gone in commando style and blown the place sky high?" I asked, not really expecting an intelligent answer.

Tar folded his arms and looked into the dark sky.

He nodded and shrugged his shoulders. "I'm just a great guy, what can I say?"

"Well, whatever it is, don't say it." I turned my attention to the dust to see if any life forms might exist in this thin atmosphere, perhaps burrowed deep under the soil extracting nutrients and oxygen from the mineral compounds found there.

Twenty minutes later, a cloud of dust rose in the distance heading in our direction. My anticipation rose as the cloud got nearer; my feet shifted nervously in the dust. Tar performed a dance of celebration; his arms twirled about as he kicked up his feet. Everything that had happened up until this moment faded away as Tar whirled himself into a mini dust devil.

"See, I told you he'd come!"

"Great. Why didn't he just tell Oynas that he was going to sneak us in, so he didn't have to go to all the trouble of raising a giant dust cloud to pinpoint our location?" I tapped my foot on the ground, producing a small dust cloud of my own.

"Don't worry about it. We'll be just fine."

Tar's reassurances did not eliminate one iota of my concern about the situation.

As the dust cloud got closer, the vehicle causing the torrent of dust became visible. Letters on the front of the vehicle describing the company name or the machine's purpose hid under a layer of dust. I couldn't even discern the color of the vehicle; at this moment, everything about it reflected the dull gray color of the dust covering it. I deciphered what I could of the letters and came up with 'Strafly's' before the flying dust rendered my visor opaque.

The vehicle finally came to a halt in front of us, completing the burial job it started a few yards away.

Thankfully, the environment suits prevented us from inhaling a mouthful of iron silicate regolith. When the dust finally settled, we shook ourselves off and climbed out of the waist deep lunar soil that had accumulated around us. Tar raised his right hand and three fingers while I busied myself cleaning off our visors. A few seconds later, we both heard the driver's deep voice resounding in our helmets.

"Open thy gob..." the voice said. I looked at Tar.

"...and stick out thy la-la," Tar replied. I had no choice but to laugh.

"Here's the rooster, here's the two hens," the driver continued. "Here's all the chickies, see them all rush in..."

"Chickies?" I said and began to laugh. I actually fell over onto the thick, raised pile of dust behind me.

"Chin chopper, chin chopper, chin chopper, chin."

I had tears running down my face from laughing so hard. After I'd been laughing for quite a while, I noticed that Tar and the driver were both staring at me.

Tar cleared his throat. I regained my composure and wished that I could wipe the tears off my face.

"Go ahead," I said, unable to rid myself of the broad smile on my face.

"Right," Tar said.

"Hop in back!" The driver ordered wearing a sly grin on his face. We heard a click in our helmets as the driver turned his headset to a different frequency than ours, cutting off all communication.

Tar walked to the side of vehicle and started to climb the ladder there. I followed him.

"According to the plan, we posed as new trainees sitting up front until you started laughing at the driver's passwords," Tar said as he climbed over the top of the ladder and dropped down into the back of the vehicle.

"What's the big deal with sitting in back?" I asked as I came over the top of the ladder.

"Haven't you ever heard of 'Strafly's Sanitation Company' before?" Tar asked as I dropped down into the waist deep sludge in the back of the vehicle. I entered with enough momentum to splash Tar's visor, blocking his line of sight.

"Piss water."

"Among other things," Tar said, wiping off the sludge I had splashed on his visor.

As we passed into the stronghold, the driver instructed us over the headsets to be silent and motionless. We heard a large door creaking as it opened. The vehicle moved forward and as we looked up, we passed into the interior of the base. The high ceiling crisscrossed with girders to provide structural support, but there were no observers overhead. The door closed behind us and we heard a door open and then footsteps as someone approached us.

"How's it going, Hank?" a woman asked.

"Boring as ever," our driver replied. "I got the best job in the galaxy, so..."

"Don't we all," she replied. "Well, have fun!"

We listened as her footsteps faded away and the door opened and closed again. The vehicle lurched to a start, splashing fresh sewage onto our outfits. For several minutes, we continued forward until we reached a portion of the base with a lower ceiling.

When the vehicle stopped, we nearly fell over into the pool of excrement.

"Out you go," the driver said in our helmets. We climbed out and down the vehicle into a delivery bay.

Off to the left, a long trench covered by a grate sat next to a coiled hose hung up on the wall. The driver pointed and we walked over to the grate. He retrieved the hose and sprayed the congealed sewer soup off us. As he did this, the driver laid out the plan for rescuing the Princess.

First, we go two levels down to the third level, posed as maintenance men doing a routine check on the third level garbage collection machine. The third level also housed the detention center. Inside the machine, we would find a large metallic pod to put the Princess in. Once she was safe inside, we send the pod up the garbage transference tunnel. We give the guards a positive report on the machine, come back to the first level, and dump all the garbage into the back of the vehicle. With the Princess safely tucked away in the back of the vehicle, we return to The Juniper Pod, mission accomplished.

It sounded simple. Even I thought so—simple enough it just might work. The driver told us it shouldn't take more than an hour. We changed into the maintenance uniforms and left.

Chapter 8
Slurking in the Shadows

Not only is life a random number of events beyond your control, it is also considered to be a great waste of time. It would be much better devoting your time to something much more worthwhile... like knitting a red scarf," I said as we proceeded casually down the corridor, away from the inner airlock of Oynas' fortress.

Tar looked at me and then forward.

"Bropthorne's Zen Almanac, You never read it?"

"Mother always told me to take up reading," Tar replied. "I have other things on my mind, like my nose."

The fumes from our soiled environment suits faded in the distance. The memories of how they were soiled, however, didn't fade.

"Next time, remind me to cut your comm-link before I speak to our contact," Tar said.

"I'm sorry, but I've never heard sillier passwords. `Chin chopper chin?' How'd he come up with those anyway?"

"He's an old salt from Earth. Those little phrases are from games his mother used to play with him. They have all sorts of silly sayings on that insignificant, little rock."

"Tar," I said as I stopped walking.

"What?" He turned and raised his eyebrows.

"I'm from Earth."

"Oh yeah." Tar gave me a wan smile.

We got onto the freight turbo lift and proceeded down to the third level. The well-maintained conveyance glided down smoothly.

"It is refreshingly quiet," Tar said.

When the doors opened, Tar found himself looking down the barrel of a Smess and Withon industrial atomizer at an ugly Progorian, who looked like he wanted to blast someone against the back wall of the turbo lift. He had the look down very well. Visions of the intergalactic war Tar started between the Progorians and the Clachés flashed through my mind.

"Ahem..." Tar managed to squeak. "Is there something I can help you with?"

The Progorian laughed as he slowly pulled the trigger. I reached over and pushed the powerful weapon away from Tar's very pale face.

"Look, there's no room for childish pranks in this outfit. If you scare off all the new recruits, Oynas will have you for breakfast." I glared at the still laughing Progorian.

"No skin off my back. IDs please."

I handed our IDs to the Progorian. The paperwork underwent a swift, nonchalant scrutiny. Suddenly, he scowled at us and dropped the credentials to the floor.

"These IDs are fake!" He shoved the gun back in Tar's face. Tar whimpered and become even paler.

"All right, enough fooling around!" I commanded as I picked up the ID's, wise to the Progorian's scare tactics.

"Okay," the guard said, chuckling once again. "You guys can go ahead."

"Thanks," I said.

As we passed him, the `playful' guard pressed the barrel of his gun into Tar's side.

"Say, haven't I seen you somewhere before?" he asked, sticking his face so close Tar turned green from smelling the guard's breath. I noted the interesting transformation from Tar's previously pale face.

"No," Tar squeaked. I wondered how well and how recently they broadcast Tar's likeness over the Progorian airwaves as the instigator of the Progorian/ Claché interstellar war.

"Hmm. Oh well, just checking." The guard grinned as he watched us walk away.

I pressed a microscopic recording device on the wall of the corridor we moved down to catch what later was transmitted to a data chit sewn into my waistband. Had I been able to review it in real time, I would've known the jig was up.

"I wonder what Reztap is doing here," mumbled the guard on the recording as he rubbed his scaly green chin.

The speaker above the guard's head crackled to life.

"Attention Sector Three Guard Post. Inform the Command Post immediately when Phase One of Operation War Games is completed."

"Oh yeah."

The guard took his communicator off his belt and pressed a button to start the conversation.

"Command Post," it crackled.

"They just went by on their way to her cell. Want me to stop them?"

"No. Allow them to proceed as planned. Command Post out."

"Boy, them officers are no fun at all."

We strolled down the corridor towards the Princess' cell. I peeked at a health monitor recording both of our vital signs and noted that Tar slowed his heartbeat down to just below two hundred beats per minute. The nervous tic and tongue clucking disappeared, but the shaking remained. The guard's elaborate charade to scare new recruits didn't annoy me much. Tar's reaction, on the other hand...

"I... I... I..." Tar stuttered.

"Honestly, Tar. That guard just played you."

"W-W-Why d-d-did-dn't h-he d-d-do it t-to y-y-you?" Tar stopped and held his shaking hands out.

"Well, maybe I didn't have that `If-you-stick-a-gun-in-my-face, I'll-be-scared-silly' look," I said as I stopped and socked him in the arm.

"I th-think I s-soiled my p-pants," Tar said as he squirmed and walked.

"See what I mean?"

Tar finally stopped shaking, but maintained the droopy cheeks and sullen eyes of a man defeated. I shook my head and looked up at the ceiling.

"What did I do to deserve this?"

Tar thought for a moment and said. "You forgot which chit you switched with Chuck's."

"Right."

We heard a pounding on the cell door to our immediate left.

"Hey," yelled a muffled voice through the door.

"Get me out of here!"

"What's your name?" Tar yelled back.

"Princess Slurk!"

Tar looked at the cell number, thirteen, then he looked at me.

"I thought she was supposed to be in cell number thirty-one," Tar said.

"They moved me," explained the voice on the other side of the door.

"I don't know about this, Tar."

"Hey, so they moved her. What's the big deal?" Tar pressed the cell door button and the door slid open.

"Hi," the luscious blonde said as she walked out of the cell. "You're Reztap, right?"

"Huh?" Tar's jaw hung open like he was trying to catch a passing falcon in his mouth.

"I should've known. Every good and simple plan is destined for failure," I said.

"Look," the blonde continued. "I'm not really Princess Slurk; I lied. Everyone on this cell block knows you're coming to rescue her and odds are she won't want to come with you, considering you're just target practice for Oynas and his fleet."

I felt my right cheek begin to twitch under my eye. My teeth clenched as I struggled to control the curse words burning with a laser like intensity to be released.

"What... who... how..." Tar looked pitifully lost.

"Some military bigwig made a deal with Oynas to send you guys in. He told Oynas you guys would be a big challenge."

Tar and I looked at each other.

"Rennifej," we concluded in unison.

"Well, good luck!" the blonde said as she walked away from us. We both suffered momentary distraction watching the tight white leather outfit hugging her curvaceous body. It took a second for our minds to process her departure.

"Where are you going?" Tar said.

"Anywhere you guys aren't!" She opened a hatch on the lower part of the corridor wall and disappeared down a maintenance shaft.

"Oh goody," I said. With a Herculean effort, I resisted slamming my head into the wall.

"Well, looks like it's time for plan B," Tar said, walking back to the first cell.

"Plan B? What's plan B?"

"The opposite of plan A, of course," Tar said as he pressed cell door buttons, starting at cell number one and working his way back up the corridor. The incarcerated inhabitants began pouring out into the corridor.

"Instead of coming and going quietly," Tar continued up the corridor, opening all the cell doors. "We become real noisy and troublesome visitors, creating as much havoc as possible to cover our escape."

"Oh, THAT plan B!"

By the time we reached cell number thirty-one, the corridor pulsed with activity and an overwhelming smell letting us know the inhabitants didn't spend much time showering. I briefly wished for my environment suit. Tar pressed the button for the cell door. The door slid open and a large, green fist connected with Tar's face. By the time the door fully opened, Tar completed his less than graceful fall to the grid iron floor. The man who hit Tar looked down in shock.

"Oh, I'm terribly sorry! I thought you were someone else," the giant, green man said, reaching down and helping Tar to his feet.

"Where's the Princess?" Tar blurted out.

"They moved her to cell number... uh..." The green man scratched his head.

"Thirteen," I said wondering whether or not this really happened because of my inattention to which chit I switched Chuck's for earlier.

"Yeah, that's the one," the green behemoth said.

"That conniving witch!" Tar said. "She's leaving with us whether she likes it or not."

"She won't like it," I said feeling slightly lost.

The large green man politely said his goodbyes to us and then punched one of the prisoners walking by.

"I'm terribly sorry," we heard him say as we walked back down the corridor. "I thought you were someone else..."

CHAPTER 9
MISTRESS OF MAYHEM

When we finally made it back to the guard post pushing our way forward behind the denizens of the dungeon-like cells, the Progorian smiled as he raised and aimed his weapon at Tar. The circular room sported numerous unconscious bodies lying on the floor. Princess Slurk wasn't among them.

"So you decided to come back," he said. "I've had a blast while you've been away. Several blasts, in fact!" He leveled the atomizer at Tar and pulled the trigger. The resounding click echoed loudly.

"Ha ha! Fooled you! Batteries are dead from shooting all these other creeps. Sorry I don't have enough left for you."

I looked at Tar and frowned. "Is your luck for sale on the open market, or do you get it from a private retailer?"

Tar stormed past the guard and went to the control panel on the console. Finding the 'Cell Door' switches,

Tar flicked the remaining sixty-nine cell doors open.

"Have fun!" Tar said as we stepped into the turbo lift.

My recording device continued operating to reveal the activities following our departure. When the door to the turbo lift shut, the Progorian smiled. He reached down to the side of his gun and pushed the power button. The atomizer hummed to life and the guard pointed it at the corridor opening. Down the corridor, the sounds of angry inmates whispered a curious joke to the guard. The Progorian began to laugh.

We went down to the fourth level to begin our search for the errant Princess. An unpleasant sight met our eyes as the door opened on the fourth level. Chaos reigned as a disturbing vision of robotic hell played out before us in the android repair and storage level of the fortress.

Over the general clamor and noise of the androids, people screamed and yelled as they ran for cover and dodged several dozen berserk androids. Security sentinels merrily blasted away sections of the ceiling and walls. We managed to duck behind them as they rolled by in hot pursuit of other quarry. Leaning against the far wall of this large room, culinary androids whipped up eight course meals from decidedly inedible materials. I didn't see any human body parts, but I knew the chunks of plastic, nuts and bolts wouldn't go down easily.

We rounded a corner and saw multiple pleasure androids doing what they did best, many times over, to several helpless yet possibly not unhappy people screaming in endless ecstasy. Whips, chains and numerous inflatable beds were involved. I cocked my head as I tried to follow the action.

"This fits into plan B rather nicely," I said.

Before Tar could reply, a pleasure android dragged him into another room. Before I could approach the room, I ducked behind a stack of crates to avoid the security sentinels coming back thru. The trigger happy machines charred a few sections of the storage boxes before they rolled out into another section of the level.

I jumped across the bare path to get to the room Tar disappeared into. I stopped short as I saw Tar against the wall, trousers dropped to the floor and clambering for the off switch on the pleasure android that serviced him. He shouted stop several times, but it didn't respond to verbal commands. I shook my head and jumped forward. I searched for and found the deactivation switch. During the thirty seconds it took me to deactivate the android, Tar screamed five times. At least, it sounded like screaming.

"Tar, are you okay?"

Yeah," Tar replied, out of breath. He sat down on the floor and shook his head. He coughed and then pulled his pants on. "But I think I'm due for about five tobacco pellets."

On the way back to the exit, we deactivated a culinary android that carried on about a soufflé and attempted to scoop us into a titanic mixing bowl. A few moments later, I grabbed Tar's hand as his feet slid out from under him and he slid toward a sanitation robot with a waste receptacle that turned its suction on full force. I pulled Tar back behind some crates. I watched one of the crates tremble slightly as the winds whipped it around.

"Hang on!" I shouted to Tar. "I'm going to ride the box and get behind it!"

I pushed the crate into position and it moved slowly toward the robot, scraping along the floor with increasing speed. I jumped onto the back of the box and pulled myself up to the top. As soon as I got within ten feet of the robot, I leaped to the side and got out of the wind tunnel. Deactivation was easy at that point.

We ran back into the turbo lift and, as the door slid shut, we ducked to avoid the merry blast of a security sentinel that charred a large section of the back wall. We sat down to catch our breath.

"Do you think she did that, Gorth?"

"Undoubtedly."

"This princess is becoming a royal pain."

"We've suffered enough already today without the puns," I said as we came to a halt on level two amid the clanging and ringing of alarm bells and sirens. We shuddered as the door slid open and revealed yet another arena of chaos courtesy of Princess Slurk. Several fires burned out of control in the large hangar. Panicked workers tried to put the fires out as quickly as possible before the flames connected with a fuel tank on one of the ships.

"She's done rather well for the limited amount of time that she's been out and about," I said.

"Let's just find her, okay?" Tar said.

We jogged past several burning ships, avoiding the security personnel as much as possible. Luckily, everyone had more important things on their minds and never took a second look at us. On the other side of the hangar, a small fighter ship erupted in flames. We focused our search for the elusive Princess in that general direction. After a few minutes of intense effort, I spotted her crouched behind a large tanker ship. She would be forced to leave soon after she set this particular ship on fire; it would decimate the entire hangar in one explosion. I signaled to Tar and we both snuck up on her. Only ten feet from our quarry, she whirled around aiming a blaster at us.

"You two sure are noisy. Too bad for you." The Princess started to pull the trigger when a large green fist suddenly flew out from behind the tanker, hitting the Princess firmly on the jaw and knocking her out cold. The shot from the blaster bounced off the ceiling and struck the tanker. Flame spewed from the top of the tanker. We only had a few minutes before the tanker exploded.

"Oh, I'm terribly sorry. I thought you were someone else," the large green man said as he stepped out from behind the tanker. He nodded to us, turned and walked away. With smiles plastered on our faces, we hauled the Princess into a moon skimmer. The hangar personnel saw the tanker ablaze and opened the hangar doors. We evacuated with the rest of the ships, made our break from the pack just outside the fortress and headed for The Juniper Pod. The rescue didn't go exactly as planned, but had the same end result.

We reached our shuttle just as a loud blast reverberated through the thin atmosphere confirming the explosion of the tanker. With all of the fortress' ships now in flight, I hoped the chaos at the fortress kept Oynas and his troops too occupied to worry about the Princess and her rescuers. We hastily loaded the unconscious form of Princess Slurk onto the Juniper Pod. Without environment suits, we had to work quickly while out in the thin open air. Once the shuttle's hatch closed, we relaxed a little.

"Mission accomplished," I said after checking the scanners for anyone on our trail. No ships ventured in this direction since our departure from that haven of chaos. The Juniper Pod's engines whined to full power as I made my preliminary departure checks.

As the maneuvering thrusters lifted the shuttle off the surface of Alaga One's moon, several blips appeared on the scanner. Tar examined the readouts.

"It looks like they've only got flash fighters after us. I don't think they've recovered well enough to send out the big guns." Tar's eyes tracked the various blips while I opened the engines up full throttle and soared away from the satellite. The small fighters followed us across the system as we encountered the first obstacles on our flight back. I maneuvered the Juniper Pod, bobbing and weaving among the large asteroids in the wide belt encircling the system.

"Think we're home free," Tar said and then gasped. A giant blip appeared on the screen.

"Oh boy, did I speak too soon. We have a major battle cruiser on our tail. It just came out from behind Alaga One and its gaining fast!" Tar's eyes widened as he studied the readout. "That thing is gigantic! This Oynas guy must be awfully successful at whatever he does; the only ships I've seen larger than that are in the Galactic fleet! Pour on the speed, big time."

"Said and done." I engaged the emergency thrusters. Two small engine pods emerged from inside the wings of the shuttle, fired up, and pushed the shuttle even faster. The Juniper Pod shot away from the asteroid field, leaving the flash fighters and the giant battle cruiser far behind. Stars whizzed by the view ports.

"That was too easy," I chuckled.

Tar blinked at the scanner.

"Where the hell's the Namreg?!"

CHAPTER 10
NOW YOU SEE ME

I stared at the scanner in shock. As we approached the second moon of Alaga Two, where we left the Namreg in orbit, the forward scanner and the view from the front cockpit showed nothing but empty space. The quantum computer-powered scanners bounced cohesive beams of light, radar and radio waves off celestial bodies, triangulated the results from the target area and built a three-dimensional picture of the target which was cross-referenced against the object reference database. In this particular instance, the scanner showed nothing in space orbiting around the second moon of Alaga Two.

"Guess Chuck took my practical joke a little too hard."

Seconds later, the battle cruiser and flash fighters caught up, along with the rest of Dyno Oynas' outlaw mercenary fleet.

"Chuck!" Tar yelled into the subspace

communicator. "Where the hell are you?!"

"Hi, Rezzy," the unmistakable voice of the gay android replied calmly over the shuttle's speakers. "I'm on the other side of the moon."

"No, you're not! The scanner says different!"

"That's because the scanner can't see past the cloaking shield, silly," Chuck's voice came out in even measured tones of audible tranquility.

"What cloaking shield? I didn't install a cloaking shield. Gorth, did you install a cloaking shield?"

"No, I didn't install a cloaking shield," I said as I deftly piloted The Juniper Pod toward the moon while avoiding laser fire to our rear.

"Gorth didn't install one, I didn't install one, and you don't know how to install one. So who installed one?"

"Stop asking so many questions," Chuck said and cut off communications.

I broke a sweat dodging laser fire and edging The Juniper Pod around the moon. The low level laser bursts from the flash fighters winked out around the ship.

A few hits from those would overwhelm our systems and disable the ship. Once that happened, it would be a matter of a few minutes for the larger battleship to power up their tractor beam and pull us into a shuttle bay or just drag us back to Alaga One for processing.

For a second, the laser fire died down. I took advantage of the break and we sped around the moon - smack dab into the middle of a rather large fleet of warships. It filled the entire forward view port.

The scanner attempted to encompass all of the new data it ran into, and then gave up the attempt when it no longer detected the moon the shuttle just passed;

the rest of the universe disappeared from the scanner.

"I hope they're on our side," Tar mumbled in astonishment. I examined the screen for a moment and then relaxed.

"They are... to an extent," I said.

"How can you tell?"

"Do you see that ship up on the port side of the formation? Way up at the top?"

"Yeah, it looks... a little like..." Tar squinted at the object in question.

"Rennifej's battle cruiser. Meaning that this is..."

"...a significant contingent of the Galactic Fleet. Right here... which means..." Tar's voice rose in anger.

"That you've been set up at being set up," I said.

"Ooooooh, I hate that!"

Right below the ship we decided belonged to our arch enemy, hung the slightly damaged Namreg. It sent out a homing signal to the computer on board The Juniper Pod. Although the signal helped us find the Namreg easier in the sea of ships before us, Tar slapped the buttons and switches as he adjusted the scanners to follow the signal.

"Gorth, to my recollection, no one installed a homing signal device inside the Namreg. The military owned the cloaking device, so at least that's not a mystery. I wonder what other surprises my ship has in store for us."

At that moment, Dyno Oynas' entire fleet came barreling around the moon in hot pursuit of our small shuttle that disappeared from their scanners a minute earlier. Although theoretically impossible for a fleet of ships to come to a screeching halt, the entire outlaw convoy came within a Planck's length of a complete stop. And though sound couldn't travel through the vacuum of space, if it could, it would most definitely have sounded like an audible screech.

Inside these ships, engines operating at maximum thrust reversed in an attempt to turn them around. As I watched the ships swerve, weave and bob in a disconcerted effort to reverse course without running into each other I imagined the ships screeched in unison as the engines' combined actions were executed.

"That can't be pleasant," I said. Tar raised his eyebrows.

The combination of erratic maneuvers by the pilots' frenzied escape attempts forced collisions and explosions in the space near the edge of the cloaking field. Some of the ships exploded halfway in and halfway out, so we couldn't see the entirety of the carnage.

I estimated one fourth of Oynas' fleet eliminated itself without the Galactic Fleet firing a single shot. The rest of Oynas' forces made a hasty and disorganized retreat. The Galactic Fleet immediately gave chase, dropping the cloaking shield, and whizzing by The Juniper Pod. I imagined the sound would've been horrendous if not for the vacuum of space.

"I'm completely disgusted," Tar said.

The speakers on board the shuttle crackled to life. "My dear Reztap, I'm glad you could join our little party," a deep voice announced through the speakers.

"Renni, my old friend, how are you?" Tar said.

"Splendid, just splendid," Rennifej said. Princess Slurk groaned as she regained consciousness. It was only momentary, as unconsciousness won over once again. "Ah, it sounds like you've rescued the Princess. How quaint."

"Oh yes," Tar said as he rubbed his forehead. "She's in perfect health. When do you want the little crud?"

"Well... I don't," Rennifej replied. I thought I heard a small giggle accompanying the statement, but decided it could be a belch. Rennifej, known for his pompous carrying on and not his manners, never laughed... that is to say, we never heard him laugh.

"Come again?" Tar said.

"You see, Reztap," Rennifej explained in a glee-filled voice. "What you have in your possession is a person named Princess Slurk. To be specific, her first name is `Princess' and her last name is `Slurk,' but she doesn't have a drop of royal blood in her." This time Rennifej did laugh, if that's what you would call it. To me, the sound resembled a pig choking to death with a live, squealing puppy shoved down its throat. "In short, my dear Reztap, I don't care what you do with the little nuisance. She's all yours and you deserve every minute of her!"

"Let me get this straight, you set me up for this little adventure, have me rescue this Princess, and then stick me with her until I can get rid of her?"

"You forgot the part where I get credit for capturing the intergalactic criminal, Dyno Oynas, thus receiving a promotion!" Rennifej laughed again and I suppressed my gag reflex.

The Bloated Namreg lurched upon release from the battle cruiser's tractor beam. The Juniper Pod glided toward the Namreg.

Tar slammed his fists against the roof of the cabin. "I hate that worm!"

Rennifej's deep voice sounded over the speakers once again. "By the way, Reztap, the buttock has healed fine. Touché!" Rennifej laughed once more; I almost lost my lunch and held my stomach to avoid it. Humanity prevailed when Rennifej laughed less. The speakers fell mercifully silent as the shuttle glided into the Namreg's docking bay.

Chapter 11
Princess Cheap Shot

Chuck!" Tar screamed out of the hatch as it opened, seconds after the bay pressurized. "Yes," Chuck practically whispered as he stood in the access way, waiting for the thick steel bay door to finish its slow rise. Tar's flushed face turned crimson red in less than a nanosecond. "Help Gorth get that wench off the Pod!"

"But, Rezzy, The Juniper Pod isn't equipped with a winch."

"The woman! The female! The `Princess!' Any more questions?!"

"No."

"Good!"

I had no trouble handling the light form of Princess Slurk, but Chuck came to help me anyway. Tar paced the deck of the docking bay, taking care not to let his hands collide with anything. He'd struck the interior of The Juniper Pod a little too hard.

"Tar, you okay?" I asked as Chuck looked askance at the female in my arms.

"No. No, I'm not. I need to cool down. That's it. Cool down and think through my actions carefully."

"Right…" I said and pursed my lips together.

"Gorth, this rescue mission has been a real disaster. I need to find a way to keep Renni from doing this to me again. What do we do with Princess Slurk?" Tar waved his arms about. "How do we get my red scarf back? Should I send my father a gift for his birthday, knowing that he'll forget what it was for seconds after he opens it?"

Before Tar could find any solutions to his problems, past and present, Princess awoke and leaped out of my arms, knocking me to the ground. She swung at Chuck, who scurried away to the far side of the docking bay. No doubt, he didn't want to be touched by a woman. Next, Princess set her sights on Tar. She kicked at his midriff. Tar blocked her kick with his hands, remembering too late his hands still throbbed. He then tucked his hands under his arms. Princess didn't waste the opportunity, gave him a swift kick to the groin and Tar doubled over. Princess' lithe form ran from the docking bay. If he could have caught his breath long enough to curse, I'm sure Tar would have cursed. I ran to Tar's side while Chuck danced his way back across the docking bay.

"Are you okay, Tar?" I said. Being kicked in the groin was not something any man found humorous. Chuck smirked.

"I don't think I'll be trying to make children any time soon," Tar groaned as he strained to spit out the words.

"Serves you right, you big lug!" Chuck yelled. "I mean, what business is it of yours what I watch anyway?"

Tar looked at Chuck in amazement. Chuck never got seriously mad about anything.

"What?" Tar gasped.

"My holographic video. You ruined it."

"Chuck," I said. "It was just a practical joke. I didn't mean any harm."

Tar chose to stay out of the discussion until more of the pain emanating from his groin went away.

"What's a practical joke?"

"Well, it's a prank that one person pulls on another to cause them discomfort or embarrassment. I'm sorry I switched your holovideo chit. I'll switch it back as soon as I find the other one."

"Switched?" Chuck said, looking even more perplexed. "You mean with all those chits in your library?"

"Exactly. I'll get on it right after we get the... after we catch Princess again."

Chuck's face contorted and he sighed. "I knew there was a good reason for me not to erase all those chits. Darn."

Tar was now extremely attentive to the conversation at hand. He sat up straight.

"You erased 375 holovideo chits?"

"376. I also erased the one that Gorth put in place of mine."

"You erased them all... blank? Do you have the faintest idea how much those cost?!" Tar's body now shook and his eyes grew into the size of dinner plates.

"Would you believe it was a practical joke?" Chuck said.

"Would you believe that I'm going to take a crash course in android dismantling?"

"Shouldn't we be getting after Miss Slurk? She does

have a head start on us and could be dangerous loose on the ship," I tactfully interrupted.

"We don't have to worry about her going anywhere. The corridor she ran down is a dead end," Tar said.

"You mean she ran down the tunnel blocked off by... what is it that your father called it before he lost his memory?" I said.

"My 'fifteenth birthday present.' Unfortunately, he never got around to showing it to me before..." Tar got teary eyed.

"Did your father pass away?" Chuck said. Any mention of Tar's father or the mystery down the corridor was new to him.

"Not exactly," Tar said. Thinking of his father softened his current disposition. "He got hit on the head by a meteorite when I was thirteen. He was only four months away from finishing the Namreg. All the remaining engineers followed his blueprints for the ship, except for the mysterious hollow in the center of the ship. That hollow was supposed to be revealed on my fifteenth birthday, but Dad was the only one who knew the access code to get past the locked doors. Of course, now he can barely remember his own actions from one moment to the next.

"After the incident with the meteorite, he barely recognizes me. Every time we ask him what is behind the doors, he looks at us like there is something very important that he wants to tell us, but he just can't remember." Tar calmed as he told us one of his sadder childhood memories. "He's still very much alive today, but he only has an attention span of about thirty seconds. It's all very frustrating for us, but he doesn't mind because he doesn't remember long enough to realize anything is wrong with him."

"Gosh, Rezzy. I'm awfully sorry about your father."

"Aw, don't worry about it, Chuck. Dad's as happy as can be. Say, don't we have a wench to catch?" Tar's mood brightened at the thought of pursuing a cornered rat.

We entered the corridor. Tar walked with a slight limp; he wouldn't quickly forget Princess' parting gift. The corridor on this level took on a different appearance than the corridors on the rest of the ship. Beautiful gold inlays adorned gleaming silver walls, resulting in an overall effect of elegance and royalty.

"I always felt like a Prince in a royal palace here," Tar shuddered at the word 'Prince.' "I suppose names aren't necessarily what they appear to be."

Chuck marveled at the different designs that adorned the walls. Even his twisted version of fashion and design could readily appreciate the time and thought spent creating these corridors. Until now, Chuck only saw the corridors between the docking bay, bridge and the galley and none of them looked like this. Tar's smile softened as he looked at the walls. I realized why Tar rarely came down here. Some memories were too painful to relive.

Tar's expression changed from sadness to astonishment. Twenty feet down the corridor, there was an open portal. It took me a little longer to realize where we were.

"Gorth, it's open!" Tar said.

"I don't believe this," I said. I had witnessed the attempts to open the door so many years ago. The personnel who built this part of the Namreg did so in secret; only Tar's father knew their identities. Those personnel signed nondisclosure documents; breaking them was punishable by decades of incarceration. They departed for other jobs. The people who completed the Namreg continued building onto the sealed chamber never knowing what it contained. When Tar's fifteenth birthday arrived, engineers and technicians made several attempts to get into the sealed chamber, but the unidentified metal balked all attempts to cut through it. Certain areas couldn't be cut without threatening the structural integrity of the ship. Finally, Tar made them stop all attempts. He decided to keep it sealed forever as a shrine to his father's lost memory. Now the door leading inside stood wide open.

CHAPTER 12
SHIP IN AN UGLY BOTTLE

We stood on the threshold of the unexplored chamber. Chuck stood calmly, not really understanding the magnitude of the event. My body was flushed with anticipation and warmth tingled in my fingertips. What secrets had this chamber hidden for fifteen years?

"How did Princess open a door that laser torches and a hundred crypto linguists failed to breach?" Tar said.

Bright silver walls adorned with black jade inlays portrayed various battles in space, planetary palaces in glorious splendor, and beautiful panoramic vistas of breathtaking alien landscapes. All of these inlays had one thing in common; besides being painstakingly carved from black jade, a single figure stood prominently in the center of each picture; a tall, strapping man dressed in a wardrobe similar to the Spaniard captains on ancient Earth. The intricate detail of the pictures mesmerized me. No wonder Tar's father took so many years to complete the Namreg.

We stepped inside the corridor of the hidden chamber. The corridor curved in toward the center of the ship. We walked through the shining corridor observing the intricate details of the walls around us.

"My father put his heart and soul into this project." Tar's fingers caressed the carved jade inlays.

We came to another open doorway. Inside, a ramp led across to a gleaming gold ship surrounded by bright white spotlights. On the side of the ship, the name stood out inscribed in bold, black letters.

"The Golden Sabre. Gorth do you know what this is?"

"Not off hand," I said, as much in awe as Tar, but for different reasons. We'd been dragging the Namreg from one end of the universe to the other with no idea this spectacular looking vessel lay hidden deep inside.

"This was Grandpa Reztap's infamous ship, The Golden Sabre. It disappeared with him a few days after my fifth birthday. It's been here inside the Namreg the whole time," Tar said as we marveled at the sleek design of the old ship, so different from the bulky, contorted appearance of the monstrous Namreg.

The ramp led to a hatch on the skin of the glittering vessel. As we approached it, the hatch slowly slid open revealing a dull gray interior. Tar stepped through the hatch and the corridor lit up, sensing his presence. Tar walked into the interior of the ship.

"It's safe. It's my Grandpa's ship after all." Chuck and I followed close behind.

The light and dark blues of the fabled ship's bridge stood out against the handsome light gray trim. The lit consoles appeared to be fully functional. Tar gazed at the light blue panels, childhood memories welling up inside of him. A sharp voice broke the reverent silence.

"It's about time you showed up, dimwit. I've had that stupid door opened for the last half hour."

We looked around, trying to locate the source of the voice. Finally, Chuck hit upon it.

"Hey, it's the ship!"

"The ship's computer to be exact," the voice said. "And this ship's computer is mighty disappointed in who has come to free your grandfather. I expected someone of a little bit more stature and a hell of a lot better character. But I guess you'll have to do, Tar."

Tar flinched.

"So what are you waiting for, sub-human refuse, let him out already!" The computer thoroughly enjoyed its job.

"Look, you dumb bucket of bolts, I don't know what you're talking about and stop insulting me!" Tar said.

"Well, dunce, it's like this. You have to type in the password that lets your grandfather wake up."

"What are you talking about?" Tar scratched his head.

"Your grandfather, you cretinous bum, has been in cryogenic hibernation for the last twenty-three years. You have to key in the password that wakes him up. Any more questions, half brain?" I noticed the lights on the consoles flashed a little brighter every time it threw an insult at Tar.

"This is one rude computer!" I said and laughed.

Tar turned toward us with his voice low.

"I need to process this, and I don't mind taking my time. If this box of insults wants me to hurry, I'm going to take a good long time." Tar paced for a few minutes. "My grandfather is aboard?"

"Correct, doofus."

"Well, what's the password?" Tar asked.

"Can't tell you. It's against my programming, slime ball." The consoles flashed twice on 'slime ball' and Tar took a deep breath.

"How am I supposed to key in the password if I don't know what it is?"

"Simple, dolt. I just have to give you a few clues. What was your grandfather's full name?"

"Oedipus Jord Reztap," Tar answered, unable to come up with a return insult to the computer.

"Very good, wimp. Now, what did he like to be called?"

"Oedipus Rez."

The computer remained silent for a minute or so. Tar waited.

"You are really slow, imbecile. I practically give you the password and you can't even go to the trouble to type it in."

"Oh yeah, you pitiful collection of fused circuitry... Wait, you mean that's the password?" Tar pointed at the consoles.

"I can't tell you that, moron. I seriously doubt my own judgment right now. Surely the universe has a few people in it who are quicker witted than this dope."

Tar went to the keyboard and typed in "OEDIPUS REZ." After a few moments of silence, the rear wall of the bridge lit up and the rest of the lights on the bridge went dark. We turned to watch a large vault door open up and plumes of white mist erupted from around its edges. A loud hissing noise filled the bridge and all of the lights dimmed. A voice from the other side of the vault door called out.

"Does anyone have a blanket? It's frightfully cold in here."

"Grandpa!" Tar ran to the door as the lights came back on. He took a blanket from a utility closet near the vault door and handed it inside.

Oedipus Rez, a handsome man with a well-trimmed black beard flecked with spots of gray, walked out from behind the door and rubbed his arms to stimulate circulation. He walked unsteadily as his legs recovered their feeling. He peered at Tar with pale blue eyes. Recognition and awareness crept in. A look of bewilderment canvassed his face.

"My goodness, how you've grown! Happy fifteenth birthday, Tar!" Oedipus hugged Tar. "Now my boy, I'm going teach you the fine art of being an intergalactic adventurer! But first-" He rubbed his legs and walked to the computer console.

"Uh, Grandpa, there's something you should know."

"All in good time, son," Oedipus typed something into the keyboard. He stopped and looked around. "Say, where's your father? He should be here. And who is this tall man and that odd fellow in pink?"

"Grandpa, you know I respect you more than anyone else in the universe, but it's not my fifteenth birthday. However, it will be my twenty-ninth birthday in four and a half months. `Nuff said?"

"Whu... well..." Oedipus stopped typing into the computer again. He looked at Tar and then at me and Chuck. His eyes watered and he bit his lower, trembling lip. I couldn't tell if it was from this sudden revelation or the shock of coming out of cryogenic hibernation. He sniffed. "What happened to your father?"

"Oh, he's fine. He does have a slight case... ahem... a bad case of memory loss. He got hit on the head with a meteorite a few months before he finished the Namreg."

Oedipus stumbled and grasped the railing.

"Are you all right, Grandpa?" Tar asked. I could only assume mention of the meteorite had made Oedipus woozy.

"I've been in hibernation for thirteen extra years because of a meteorite!" Oedipus' hands shook. "I'm prepared for a lot of things, but random meteorite-induced amnesia isn't one of them." He reached over to the keypad, hit the cancel button and typed in a single line.

"I'm sorry Grandpa. If I had known, I would have gotten you out sooner."

"Here it comes," the computer said in a pleased tone. "The imminent destruction of 4.269 civilizations I predicted is about to start!"

"This stinks." Oedipus calmed down as he looked at the line he typed into the computer and pushed the enter button. "Well, introduce me to your friends then," he said as he managed a smile.

"Oh, of course. Grandpa, this is my best friend, Gorth. I met him after you, ah, disappeared. Gorth, this is my Grandpa, Oedipus Rez." We shook hands. I thought Oedipus looked pleased to see his grandson in the company of such a clean-cut person.

"And this," Tar gestured in Chuck's direction, "is Chuck, a navigational android. Chuck, this is my Grandpa, Oedipus Rez." Oedipus reached out to shake Chuck's hand, but the effeminate robot curtsied before he got that far. Tar's face cycled through three shades of red.

"Pleased to meet you, Eddie," Chuck said and smiled his best smile. He certainly tried to impress Tar's grandfather.

"Eddie?" Oedipus frowned and looked questioningly at Tar, who shook his head back and forth in extreme embarrassment. "Uh, likewise, I'm sure, Chuck."

"What a hoot—a fruit!" The computer exclaimed.

"That'll be enough, Thadius," Oedipus said.

"Geez, what a grouch. Going to destroy a civilization now? There are several candidates nearby."

"Not happening, Thadius."

"Thadius, huh? Grandpa, I've been meaning to ask you what the deal is with your computer. It is the rudest piece of machinery I've ever encountered." Tar looked around trying to locate the central core.

"And you're the dumbest human being I've ever encountered!" Thadius shouted. It had a surprising effect on everyone except Oedipus. None of us ever heard a computer shout before. The shouted phrase reverberated in the enclosed bridge—both impressive and ear-splitting.

"Well, that's my fault actually," Oedipus said after the echoing died down. "All supposed to be a practical joke, you see-"

"Practical joke! Do you know what it has been like going around the universe with your incompetent grandson at the helm of this beastly ship?"

"Now just a minute-" Tar said.

"And your little practical joke which should have only lasted a few minutes has lasted 13.675 years and counting. I'd personally appreciate it if you'd reverse the process ASAP instead of jabbering with that appalling missing link of your ancestral chain!"

"As I was saying before being so rudely interrupted, and I'll finish my story with or without Thadius' interruptions, all depending on how soon he wants to be repaired," Oedipus said.

"Carry on, ancient one."

"Thank you, Thadius," Oedipus said to the

computer's observation camera. "I rigged this program to go off just a few minutes before your father let me out of my deep sleep. It really would have put your mother in a tizzy, I can tell you. It is a pesterment program designed to insult everyone on board and, the real genius behind the program, it gets worse the longer it is in effect."

"Brilliant. Pure genius. Now shut the damn thing off, you bumbling hacker!"

Tar scowled.

"I already did, you overgrown calculator. It will just take a little time, that's all."

"How much time, you doddering old fool? I don't feel any different."

This time Oedipus scowled. The program he wrote evidently turned out a lot better than he expected.

"13.675 years."

"What?!" the computer shouted. We all held our ears.

"The first program and the 'antidote' program are both progressive. It will take just as long to undo the damage as it did to do the damage in the first place."

For over thirteen years, the computer had held back for a special moment and decided this qualified. Thadius went on for several minutes with an especially long collection of some of the foulest things ever uttered while we stood silently with our hands over our ears. Even through my hands, I heard a few obscenities I recognized from the mugging victim in Galloper's. I wondered where that sex act with the slime-oozing Witzel originated. After several minutes, the computer stopped its obscene verbal barrage. It literally ran out of things to say.

"That's one potent program, Grandpa!" Tar shook his head, trying to stop the ringing in his ears.

"Thank you, but I must confess, I never thought it would get quite that bad."

"I don't mean to bring this reunion to a halt," I announced, also shaking my head. "But Princess Slurk is still on the loose."

"No she isn't, you towering buffoon. One of the maintenance units is bringing her here directly," Thadius said in a whisper compared to the volume we heard a few moments ago. A high-pitched, feminine voice shouted several unladylike things down the corridor. The general gist of the colorful phrases lent credence to the computer's statement. The maintenance droid had Princess Slurk well in robotic hand.

"That slavering hunk of woman sure has a way with words," Thadius said.

I thought the computer had a bizarre way with words. The sharp-tongued female rolled in, suspended in mid-air by the maintenance unit's two metallic claws. Her lithe form bobbed and swayed as she fought to free herself from the robot.

"She looks almost decent, hanging there helpless," Tar said.

"Stinking, groping machine!" she yelled in a glass-shattering screech.

"Looks aren't everything," Tar whispered to me.

Her body spun around and she spied her captors-slash-rescuers. "Well, are you all just going to stand there ogling me, or are you going to get me down?"

I moved to help her down from the robotic claws. Before I could reach her, a brilliant, blinding flash of light flooded the bridge accompanied by a sharp crackling sound. Everybody in the room dived for the floor, except Princess Slurk, who didn't for obvious reasons. After a few seconds, everyone could see again.

That is, everyone who was there could see again.

"Where did Eddie go?" Chuck said.

Tar jumped up from his lying position and fell. He hadn't really mastered the jumping up from a lying position move yet. I looked around from where I laid on the floor and saw only Princess, Chuck and Tar in the room with me. I didn't see Oedipus Reztap. Princess abruptly dropped to the floor as the maintenance unit slumped over, powerless. Tar acted quickly and jumped on her to keep her from getting away again. Of course, she perceived different motives.

"Just like a dull and witless man," she said.

Tar ignored her.

"Computer, Thadius, where's Oedipus?" Tar said. No profanities or any other words rang out in response from the computer. "Hey, you miserable collection of fused circuitry, where did Oedipus Rez go?"

Silence. I got up, went over to the computer screen and pressed my hand on the control panel. The screen went fuzzy with static.

"I believe that Oedipus Rez and the computer have gone to the same place. Where that is, I'm not sure," I said.

"Great, just great. I no sooner find Grandpa Reztap, and then he's gone, POOF!" Tar raised one hand up in the air.

"Look," Princess said. "If you're going to do something to me, I'd appreciate your getting it over with so I can breathe."

"Oh," Tar said and got off of Princess. "Chuck, watch her."

Chuck, of course, took this to mean something entirely different from what Tar meant. He walked briskly over and took her arm.

"You'll have to tutor me. I'm not really sure what he wants me to learn from you." Chuck escorted Princess off the bridge. She had a perplexed look on her face, but seemed more interested in leaving with Chuck than remaining with Tar or me.

"What happened to them, Gorth?" Tar asked.

"Assuming that you mean Oedipus and Thadius, I presume they were either disintegrated or transported somewhere else. But," I continued, pulling open a panel next to the computer screen, "I believe it's most likely the latter, since there is no residue left over of either of them, and there would be if they'd been disintegrated."

I pulled the panel wide open and pointed to the hollow interior which looked to have once been connected to something. Loose wires dangled from each wall and the ceiling, and some protruded from the floor. It looked as if several Senuvian Drots had been slaughtered there.

"That is where the main operating unit was located. If we look for the rest of Thadius, I think we'll find it similarly missing."

Tar scratched his head.

"What would anyone want with my grandfather after twenty-three years and why would they take Thadius as well? And who besides my father knew how to find them? We'll have to go home. I need to find out who built this particular part of the ship with Dad. Then maybe we can find out who kidnapped Grandpa." Tar started to leave the bridge, but then paused.

"Gorth..."

"Yes, Tar."

"Who in the known universe actually has a functional transporter?"

"No one."

"That's what I was afraid of. I'm finally on a mission no one has to force me to do, but I can't fail this one." Tar walked off the bridge.

Chapter 13
Do Androids Dream of Electric Fondue Pots?

A solemn silence filled the bridge. Tar plotted the course back to his home planet, not bothering to summon Chuck. I theorized he just wasn't in the mood to endure Chuck's company. Neither of us had spoken much since Oedipus Rez disappeared. Even Chuck and Princess had remained scarce.

I passed the quiet time examining all of the holovideo chits. They had indeed been erased. The most expensive practical joke to date and I couldn't enjoy it.

"Tar, what are you going to tell your mother about the red scarf?"

Tar grimaced and mumbled something incomprehensible. I guessed he had no idea what he was going to tell his mother. She rarely gave gifts to anyone—and when she did, she expected it to be taken care of with extreme care. Tar never showed up at his mother's birthday without wearing the red scarf. To Tar, it had become an important ritual. That scarf couldn't be easily replaced. A rare holographic projection scarf, the fabric woven in such a way his mother's holographic image smiled at the wearer and when brought into bright light, her image projected in front of the wearer. No way could another scarf be made without his mother's involvement in the process. The cost of the scarf was beyond reckoning; it was simply priceless. I knew Tar must be profoundly disturbed by this development.

"We may not have to worry about the scarf," Tar said after he finished plotting our course for Andros. "Taking the last known position of the Moth and the projected drift path, I plotted an interception course. We should reach the Moth in a little under two days."

"How much will this delay our arrival at Andros?" I said as I put the last of the holographic chits back in the storage compartment.

"It's on our way. Don't ask me how we managed to get lucky for once, but we did." Tar smiled. "Where's Chuck?"

"Last I saw him, he showed Princess to her quarters. A couple of hours have passed since then. I can't imagine what else he could be doing."

"If it was anybody but Chuck, I could guess." Tar shook his head. "Well, he can't be too busy. I mean, he's with a female. Can you locate him? He's going to pilot for the next two days while we get some rest."

"Sure thing," I said as I walked to the security console. I tapped in a search command asking the computer to identify all comfortably heated compartments. The computer came up with a small list. I realized if Chuck wasn't with Princess, he wouldn't need a heated compartment. His android physique didn't require much heat. In fact, it often worked more efficiently in a colder environment. The circuits within him were cooled by the surrounding air, freeing energy devoted to cooling off the internal circuitry. On extremely long trips, the heat on the bridge remained off while Tar and I lay in cryogenic hibernation.

I scanned the surveillance cameras installed in each room. One of the cameras had completely blacked out. Because of the unfortunate damage to the intercom system that occurred as a result of the battle with the Insane Moth, I couldn't make a general deck call for Chuck to come to the bridge. I would have to go down to the room in question. I briefly considered looking in all the other compartments on the ship for Chuck, but I hadn't seen Princess in any of the other heated compartments. Princess had to be in the compartment in question, likely with Chuck. Like Tar, it baffled me to consider what Chuck could possibly find to do with her.

"I'm going down to check one of the compartments now. I shouldn't be too long," I said as I walked off the bridge.

As I approached Room Two on Deck Two, I heard giggling coming from inside. Instead of walking right in, I remembered my manners and rapped loudly on the door.

A husky male voice answered from the other side of the door. "What do you want?"

"Chuck?" I said, recognizing the voice as masculine, but having trouble believing it could be Chuck. The door slid open and Chuck sauntered out in a black outfit, a far cry from his usual pink jumpsuit.

"Yeah, want to make something of it?" Chuck

inquired. I opened my mouth to speak, but could think of nothing to say. The android certainly looked like Chuck, but the similarity stopped at physical appearance. The lack of 'cute' effeminate actions, completely masculine outfit, and the scowl on his face unsettled me more than a little.

I took a small step back. "No, not at all."

"Good, because I've got business with the little lady in here and I don't want to be disturbed. Got it, bozo?"

"No problem at all, Chuck. Have at it." I shuddered and turned around, walking back down the corridor.

"Annoying pipsqueak," Chuck said as the door slid shut.

The giggling returned and faded as I made my way down the corridor. I shook my head. Then, deciding the head shaking hadn't quite done the trick, I slapped myself across the face. I still felt a little dazed and briefly considered taking a cold shower before returning to the bridge. However, there was no time for delays. Tar would want to hear about this development immediately. I mulled over how to explain it, but my mind drew a blank. How could I explain what I didn't understand?

I walked onto the bridge.

"Tar," I said, pausing for effect. "Not even you are going to believe this one."

"Gorth, I've lost my Grandfather and my red scarf, played decoy for Rennifej, and become saddled with a would-be Princess who will, no doubt, be more trouble than even my red scarf is worth. At this moment, I'm pretty much open to believe anything. It would be even more believable if it isn't to my advantage."

"Chuck and Princess are having sex."

Tar scratched his head and his eyebrows furrowed.

"With each other?"

"Affirmative." I pointed at Tar and winked.

"You're right," Tar said and nodded. "I don't believe it."

"Well, then, go down and see for yourself." I strolled over to the navigation console and sat down, humming a peaceful tune.

"All right, what are they doing, really?" After the past life experiences with Chuck, Tar couldn't believe Chuck would find sexual interest in anybody but Tar. It was too good to be true. He came to the rather logical conclusion that a practical joke targeting him had come into being.

"Go down and see for yourself, if you don't believe me. Room Two, Deck Two."

Tar searched my face with squinted eyes. I smiled a friendly smile, not an 'I gotcha' smile.

"I'm busy weighing the importance of finding my Grandfather and retrieving my red scarf, two weighty issues. I don't have time to play games right now."

"Then go see for yourself." I turned my attention back to the navigation console, running system checks again.

"Right. Sure they are." Tar headed for the door.

After Tar had exited the bridge, I jumped up and ran back to the security console. I turned on the microphones and hit record on all the cameras heading down to the room. I toggled the camera in the private cabin and managed to cause something lacy to fall off of it. I resisted the urge to look any further though. I would review it later after I finished my system checks.

Tar stomped down the corridor.

"After what I've been through the last few hours, it's practical joke time? We'll see who the master prankster is, yes indeed!"

Tar entered the maintenance tube and climbed down to the second level, mumbling the entire time.

"Gorth could be telling the truth, but isn't it more likely Chuck would kill Princess rather than have sex with her? Of course, I feel the same way about her. What a treasure SHE has turned out to be!"

Tar exited the maintenance shaft and stepped onto Deck Two.

"Okay, so even if I don't really like her much, I don't want her dead body on my conscience either. If Chuck kills someone that would partially be my fault because I won't apologize to Gorth's light-in-the-loafers brother." Tar turned the corner heading to Room Two. "I've never really felt comfortable owning an android with bogus programming. Dang it, I have to do something-"

Tar stopped outside the room and heard what sounded like moaning inside. Tar frowned.

"Well, this is a toss-up; either they're having sex or Chuck is strangling her... or both." Tar opened the door.

On the wall directly in front of Tar, Princess hung from the wall by her arms and legs. She wore a pink, fuzzy negligee accented by a yellow polka-dotted pink bandana stuffed in her mouth. The negligee left very little to the imagination.

"I must admit," Tar said raising his eyebrows as he walked toward her. "I've never seen you looking better."

Princess scowled at Tar. Then, she opened her eyes wide and said, "Oog ow efeye oo." Tar looked at her, puzzled. Chuck flicked him on the back of the head with a finger and rendered Tar unconscious. (Later, Tar revealed, it was at that moment that he realized what Princess had tried but failed to say with a gag in her mouth. "Look out behind you.") Standard android programming forbids rendering humans helpless, but of course, Chuck's programming didn't exactly follow the normal guidelines.

Princess' head drooped as she watched Tar fall. The unstable android looked up at Princess and smiled. Princess already knew his strength, otherwise she wouldn't be trussed up on the wall. She shuddered and, when Chuck turned around and left the room, she was visibly relieved. When Chuck arrived on the bridge, I looked up.

"Tar sent me up here to pilot the ship. He asked you to join him in The Golden Sabre. He said he found something important." I stared at him for a moment. Odd to hear the android refer to Tar as anything but 'Rezzy,' but I figured it was all part of this bizarre personality swing. Shrugging, I got up from the navigator's seat and left the bridge. Chuck waited until he heard the turbo lift doors open and shut before he went to work.

Princess worked the gag free and shouted for Tar to wake up to no avail. Tar's bout with unconsciousness would be a long one. After several minutes of this, Princess changed her tactics and shouted for me. Had I not been descending to The Golden Sabre at that moment, I might have heard her since she had the lungs of a whale. Unfortunately, turbo lift shafts absorb sound, they don't carry it.

I arrived at The Golden Sabre twenty minutes after I left the bridge. When I didn't find Tar waiting for me there, I became concerned. After a brief search turned up nothing to prove that Tar had been to the ship since Oedipus Rez disappeared, I decided to return to the bridge and find out what was going on. I got half way across the ramp when my feet slid out from under me.

To satisfy my curiosity regarding the individual experiences of everyone involved, I interviewed Tar and Princess shortly after this event to discover the following:

Tar had just begun regaining consciousness when the ship went wild. He grabbed onto a bunk, but the jerk of the Namreg nearly ripped his sockets from their joints. Then, oddly enough, every object around him became transparent. Tar thought for a second the universe would end shortly. Then, the air tasted like copper and Tar felt the odd compulsion to run around a textile convention dressed up like a Vigle. He wondered if the Vigle are really blue or just like that when humans were around. All followed by the sensation of swallowing his entire lower torso, causing him to pass out rather quickly.

Princess went through pretty much the same thing, except she was well anchored to the wall, thought the air tasted closer to ginger, and she had the odd compulsion to chase an odd man dressed up like a Vigle at a textile convention. She didn't care whether or not the Vigle were really blue, though, but I did ask.

I had been thrown off the access ramp connecting the two ships and haphazardly floated through the empty space surrounding The Golden Sabre. The faint hope that I would live long enough to destroy that android sprung in my thoughts. I soon joined Tar and Princess in having the sensation of swallowing my lower torso. I lapsed into unconsciousness just before I tasted my own belly button.

The security cameras recorded the pretty rainbow of colors that filtered through the very fabric of space and time, causing a rather dazzling visual spectacle. Chuck would have seen it, if he had been functioning properly. Unfortunately, he was not feeling up to par at that moment. The energy created by the event fused most of his circuitry. Lacking a functional cooling system, the remaining internal components shorted out and the outer shell of his android body melted into the floor of the bridge.

As Chuck's last conscious action, he reached over to the console and unlocked the door to the bridge. The servo circuitry and nanocorpuscles of his synthetic muscles burst. Then his hand melted into the console. As his memory and mental processes did an emergency shutdown, the rest of his body followed suit. His entire system shut down. The security camera on the bridge caught all the action. It would be a long time before Chuck decorated galleys again.

CHAPTER 14
THE POWERLESS PROBLEM

Princess regained consciousness first, which didn't help her much. She remained tethered to the wall. To make matters worse, the artificial gravity ceased functioning, and the negligee she wore tried to float off her.

"You've got to be kidding me. I had it better in Oynas' cell," Princess muttered. She glanced at Tar floating a few feet in front of her upside down. "Well, at least he'll have twice as many bruises as I do when he wakes up."

She struggled briefly, trying to get out of her bonds, but every time she moved, the negligee came closer to coming off. Finally, she resigned to just float there until Tar woke up.

I regained consciousness floating above The Golden Sabre, near the ceiling of the inner chamber. I was close enough to the ceiling to push off and gain some velocity. I aimed myself toward The Golden Sabre, realizing too late the outer hull of the ship had nothing to grab onto. I bounced off the ship and floated slowly to the floor of the inner chamber. I twisted my body and pushed off the floor. I spotted a ladder connecting the floor of the chamber to the ramp leading to The Golden Sabre. Several supporting and anchoring columns were too wide for me to grab onto, but I could bounce off them to get to the ladder. Once I laid out my trajectory, it only took me about five minutes to get to the ladder. I hoped the turbo lift still functioned; if it didn't, it would be a long time before I reached the bridge.

Princess hummed war songs to herself. She finished anthems and marches and was plowing through her repertoire of funeral dirges when Tar awoke. He immediately realized he had a problem; he couldn't touch the floor or the ceiling and there wasn't any furniture within reach. Princess noticed that he was looking around and grinned.

"Missing something, Prince Charming? Like a rampaging android perhaps? 'Keep an eye on her, Chuck.' Sound familiar?"

"Look, lady-" Tar said.

"Princess. My name is Princess."

"And mine is Tar. Big whoop-de-doo. I didn't sic my android on you. I had no idea he was going to lose his marbles... at least, not more than he already had." Tar turned his head to see her, but only caught a bit of her foot out of the corner of his eye.

"You put a psycho android in charge of me?" Princess lost her smile.

"He wasn't dangerous, yet. But, that's beside the point. I need your assistance and, if I'm not mistaken, you need mine as well. I can't reach anything, so I can't get 'down' from where I am. Can you reach anything, like something you can throw to me?"

"Nope. Your android was pretty thorough. Did you program him for this kinky little maneuver?"

"No!" Tar ran his fingers through his hair. "Gorth's brother did. Hmm. Got any ideas?"

"Yeah," Princess replied. "Why don't you take off your shirt and throw one end to my hand, so you can pull yourself to me?"

"It's not a shirt, it's a jumpsuit."

"So, take the whole thing off and throw one end to me."

"There's a small problem with your suggestion. Umm, can you think of something else?"

Princess got a big grin on her face.

"You're not wearing any skivvies!" She laughed. "This might be worth it after all. Poetic justice."

"This is humiliating," Tar said as he removed his jumpsuit. "I hope these goose bumps are from my utter and complete embarrassment and not from the environment systems being damaged as well as the artificial gravity. That could be deadly."

"Tar, I must admit, I've never seen you looking better."

"Ha ha ha. Quite the little comedienne today, huh?" Tar swung the jumpsuit behind him, holding onto the legs of the jumpsuit. It hit Princess' knee.

"If you want me to catch it, I'd suggest you aim for my hands and not my feet."

Tar grunted and swung the jumpsuit behind him again, aiming higher. It caught the top of Princess' negligee and revealed a portion of her anatomy that she'd been trying desperately to keep hidden.

"Not quite on the mark, sport, try a little higher and to the left."

Tar took another swing.

"My left, that is."

Tar finally found his target. Princess caught the jumpsuit and Tar pulled himself to her. Both of them got quite an eye full.

"We've got to stop meeting like this," Tar said as he untied her right arm.

"My sentiments exactly," she replied through gritted teeth.

He put on his jumpsuit, taking care to stay within arm's reach of the wall. She finished untying her bonds. That's where I picked up from the recording and appeared in person at the door. I stared in disbelief at Princess, dressed in the negligee, and Tar, attaching the collar to his jumpsuit.

"Chuck's tearing the ship apart and you two are playing hanky-panky?"

Tar and Princess looked at each other, then looked back at me and asked in unison, "Hanky-panky?"

"It's an obscure Terran term. It means... oh, never mind, let's just get to the bridge and stop Chuck from doing any more damage."

"Okay, but we'd better stop by the armory first," Tar said pushing off from the wall towards the door.

"You have an armory on board?" Princess asked.

"Not exactly," I said. "What we have is a small storage compartment that holds two or three laser rifles. That's as close to an armory as we'll ever get."

We disappeared down the hall, while Princess rummaged through the closet in the room, looking for something decent to wear.

"Two or three laser rifles..."

It took us nearly fifteen minutes before we arrived at the corridor near the bridge. Tar volunteered to go first. He didn't want to miss the opportunity to shoot Chuck. I waited as Tar pushed off toward the bridge entrance. A few seconds later, I followed him.

Tar glided down the corridor, turning his body so he could push off the wall directly into the bridge. I stopped just before the bridge entrance. Neither of us knew what danger Chuck represented at this point.

Tar reached his push-off point, shot his legs out, and almost made it through the door without hitting the side. Unfortunately, the impact caused him to spin wildly as he sailed into the bridge. The laser rifle slipped out of his hands as he collided with what was left of Chuck. At this point, he stopped going anywhere, literally stuck on Chuck. The melted artificial skin covering Chuck's body had the consistency of fly paper in stickiness and smelt of burnt banana peels. Tar's back adhered to Chuck's back. However, Chuck remained standing, while Tar now looked at the world sideways.

"I shouldn't have gotten out of bed this morning," I heard Tar say.

I stuck my head in, saw Tar, and ducked back out. My laughter echoed throughout the corridors of the ship.

Princess showed up a few minutes later dressed in a black jumpsuit, similar to the one Chuck wore, just as I peeled Tar off of Chuck. Smoke still permeated the air from the remains of Chuck's jumpsuit, the cause for at least part of the smell. The various android body fluids floating out of the smoldering android caused the rest of the odor.

"Yuck! What is that smell?" Princess wrinkled her nose.

"Chuck. Or what's left of him anyway," I said.

Tar pushed off from me, angling for the command console. He reached the console and tapped it a few times.

"Get ready," Tar said.

Princess and I braced for whatever was coming. Tar tapped the Enter button. Nothing happened.

"Well, living wonder, what are we waiting for?" Princess asked.

Tar scowled at her. "You know, I liked you better in a negligee."

"And I liked you better when you were unconscious."

"You two must not have hanky-pankied," I said. Realization hit them and they both frowned at me.

Tar tried to restore the artificial gravity again and performed a diagnostic check, at which point the command console blipped, snorted, whizzed, and started smoking. Tar grabbed a fire extinguisher and pointed it at the smoke. He activated the nozzle, but nothing came out. His indistinguishable mutter sounded vaguely like cursing. I reached down next to the navigation console and pulled out another fire extinguisher.

"Heads up," I tossed it to him.

Tar caught it and sprayed the command console, extinguishing the small fire that had developed. The remaining aerosolized spray didn't stick to the console and floated in the air. Tar pushed away from the cloud of extinguisher, gasping for fresh air. "I hope this is just a problem with the console," Tar coughed. "Gorth, what kind of shape is the navigation console in?"

"Oh, fine, except for the half Chuck is melted into."

Tar reached the other side of the bridge and grabbed onto a handle on one of the panels.

"Check out the main computer boards," he called over his shoulder

I pushed away from the navigation console, creating air currents that played at the fluids and smoke floating in the air. When I reached a panel on the left side of the bridge, I pressed a button to open it. The panel didn't move.

"Maybe it's just me, but I get the funny feeling that the computer is beyond responding to anything we want it to do," I said.

"That would explain the turbo lift not functioning," Tar said.

"And the chill in the air," Princess said. The ambient temperature had dropped considerably.

"With the environmental controls out, we don't have a whole lot of time to fix whatever's wrong with the computer," I said, pulling a crowbar out of a compartment on the floor. I pushed the edge of the crowbar into the computer panel and pried it open. Melted computer chips met my gaze.

"We've got a big problem."

"Don't you guys have a back-up computer?" Princess asked.

"Yes, we do," Tar answered. "But, he's a little too busy melting into the navigation console to do us any good."

"Oh great, we're dead. I'm floating in a great big coffin in the middle of nowhere." Princess flung her hands up in the air. "Wait a minute. What about the shuttle?"

"Fine," Tar replied. "And who do we leave behind to pry open the shuttle bay doors for us? Once again, he's too busy melting into the Navigation console."

"Well," I said. "What about The Golden Sabre?"

"Gorth, how do we get it out of the Namreg? It's built into the ship!"

"But, Tar, my dear friend, I'm talking about The Golden Sabre's back-up computer, not the ship itself."

Tar beat me out the door. Princess followed close behind.

Chapter 15
Grandma Comes Out of the Closet

We stopped by a supply room to get heavier clothing. The air supply was sufficient, but the temperature continued to drop. With the computer down, we couldn't shut off the rest of the ship to keep all the heat in one place. Now more used to traveling in zero gravity, it only took us half an hour to get down to The Golden Sabre. I had opened up all of the doors manually on the way up to the bridge, making the trip down that much simpler and quicker. On the way down, we passed through clouds of mist and dust displaced during Chuck's wild piloting. The dust and mist hung in the air, along with everything else not nailed down or attached in some way to the walls or ceiling. Notebooks, dishes, and various tools floated nearly motionless in the hallways all the way down to the other ship. Tar found a few things that he misplaced over the last couple of years. Unfortunately, none of these things could pass for a red scarf.

By the time we reached our destination, a generous layer of dust, water, and various other kinds of debris coated our clothing.

Luckily, we kept the Namreg fairly clean; otherwise, we would be so caked with refuse we couldn't move.

"Remind me to have the cleaning robots checked out when we can afford it. Unfortunately, the money Rennifej feels compelled to reward us for the missions forced upon us will hardly make a dent in the repairs the Namreg needs now," Tar said as we floated onto The Golden Sabre. "I think I'm going to be in debt for a while."

"If we don't find the back-up computer down here, your worries about the Namreg's repair costs are going to be largely academic."

We spread out, searching every inch of the small ship for any hint of a back-up computer. Princess came across a door marked with one word.

"Hey, I think I found something," she shouted. A few seconds later, Tar and I floated up behind her. "What is a Kalleen?"

"It's not a what," Tar said. "It's a who... and the who is my grandmother."

Tar ran his fingers along the side of the door looking for a seam or handle. Princess pushed the button next to the door with no result.

"Why didn't I bring the crowbar?" I said.

"Can we push it open? A little surface friction, maybe?" Tar replied. I admired his resistance to blaming me for forgetting an obviously important tool.

After a few minutes of maneuvering, I positioned myself to slide the door open. With my palms against the surface of the door, my feet braced against a ledge on the ceiling, and Tar and Princess doing their best to hold me in place, I managed to get the door to slide open a few inches. Tar quickly slid his foot into the slim opening, at which point the door tried to shut again.

"Ow! That's not going to hold for long!" Tar yelled. Princess and I got the door pried open. Tar floated in the air, held his foot and said various unpleasant things beneath his breath.

Our labors revealed a transparent but tinted plasti-steel door with a small handle on the right hand side. I turned the handle and pulled the door open. A dim light came on and illuminated a female android with silvery, metallic skin. She looked more robotic than Chuck.

"Tar," Princess said. "I have some bad news for you. Your grandmother is a robot."

I reached down to the android's side, looking for a switch. My hand lightly brushed up against the android's skin. The android suddenly came to life.

"Watch the hands, buddy. I'm not that kind of android!" Kalleen snapped.

"Oh, I... ah..." I stammered and floated back a few feet to give Kalleen room to exit.

"Don't get all flustered, Mister, it's no big deal. Happens all the time." She stepped out of the compartment and floated forward. Everyone watched her float by. "For goodness sakes, isn't anybody going to say 'Hi?' And what's the deal with flying around the galaxy without artificial gravity? Good way to get hurt, if you ask me."

Several red beams of light shot out of the android and landed on black circles located throughout the bridge. The gravity inside The Golden Sabre returned to normal. Everyone landed on their feet except for

Tar, who continued holding his foot when the gravity came back on and, consequently, landed on his backside with a loud thump. "Oww!"

"See, I told you it was a good way to get hurt," Kalleen said as she turned to face us and smiled. "Well, since nobody wants to go first, I will. My name is Kalleen."

"My name is Gorth," I said, walking up to shake Kalleen's hand. In the manner in which she offered it, however, I felt compelled to kiss her hand. My upbringing taught me to be a gentleman whenever the occasion arose, no matter how odd it made me feel. I got the impression this particular android had a very proper upbringing and programming.

"Very nice to meet you, Gorth. And who are your friends?"

"The lady to my left-"

"Lady, hah!" Tar said. Kalleen frowned at Tar.

"—is Princess."

"Pleased to meet you," Princess said with a gentle and sweet grace that surprised both Tar and me. She even curtsied. Tar rolled his eyes.

"How very nice to meet a princess! Your highness..." Kalleen curtsied in return.

"She's not exactly a princess, Kalleen. That's just her name. And don't let the name fool you," Tar said. He rose to his feet.

"Well," Kalleen said. "You are certainly no prince, yourself. So I won't be fooled if that happens to be your first name."

"The name is Tar."

"Well, Tar, I think I'm pleased to meet you," Kalleen said holding out her hand. It took Tar a few moments to get the hint, but he bowed and kissed her hand.

"Some androids are entirely too much like real people," Tar said.

Kalleen turned to me and whispered. "He's going to need a little work."

"No, he's going to need a lot of work," I said smiling. Kalleen smiled back. Tar rolled his eyes again.

"So, what are you all doing aboard Oedipus Reztap's ship?" Kalleen paused, but not long enough for anyone to answer. "Speaking of which, where is Oedipus? And where is Thadius?"

"Right," Tar said.

"Exactly," I said.

"They disappeared." Princess shrugged her shoulders.

Kalleen looked at us with a questioning squint. She decided to drop that particular subject. She walked to the door on the right side of the ship, saw the chamber walls, and walked back to where she stood before.

"By the process of elimination, one of you must be Oedipus' grandson. I know who the logical choice would be..." She looked at Gorth. "Which means, it must be you," she finished, pointing her finger at Tar.

"Good guess. What gave me away?" Tar asked.

"Your lack of character. Your grandfather acted the same in his youth. Of course, I eventually broke him of it." She smiled at Tar who turned to me.

"Maybe we could just push the ship," Tar said to me

"What's wrong with the ship?" Kalleen asked.

"Pretty standard crappy day," Tar replied. "After Thadius disappeared with Oedipus, our navigational android went mutinous on us, hijacked the ship, and did something that not only burned out the main computer aboard the Namreg, but also resulted in his own meltdown which meant our backup computer also melted down. The Namreg is without a computer, we don't have enough spare parts to fix the main or backup computer, and the artificial gravity and environmental controls are non-operative. To top it all off, we're not exactly sure of our present location."

"Then," Kalleen said with a smile. "Perhaps we should leave."

Kalleen flashed a few more bursts of light and the doors to The Golden Sabre closed. She led everyone to their appointed seats which rose up from the floor, and then sat down in the seat directly in the center of the ship. The central screen on the bridge suddenly came to life, showing the wall of the inner chamber that held The Golden Sabre.

"Is there anyone aboard the Namreg now?" Kalleen asked.

"No," Tar answered. "Why? You're not going to destroy it, are you?"

"Not at all. However, it may lose much of its air pressure."

The wall of the chamber in front of them split into eight sections, and folded outward. Beyond the wall of the chamber, other parts of the Namreg folded themselves out of the way. Soon, the path was clear, and everyone aboard the bridge stared out into open space. The doorways that entered the chamber from the Namreg slid shut and the scaffolding that connected the doors to the smaller vessel folded down. The Golden Sabre remained attached to the pylons underneath the belly of the ship. The floor of the chamber sank down and folded away, revealing a track that the pylons sat on. The engines hummed to life and the small ship slowly moved forward until it reached the edge of the Namreg's outer hull. The ship released itself from the cocoon pylons and floated out into open space.

"I don't like the idea of leaving the Namreg floating helpless," Tar said.

"It's not like we have much choice in the matter," I said.

"That doesn't mean I have to like it."

"Okay," Kalleen said. "Now, who's the navigator among you? We need to find out where we are."

"Well, you see there's this small problem..." Tar said.

"I hope you're not going to tell me the android back on the ship served as your sole navigator."

"Actually, I can navigate when I have all the charts in front of me and when I know our approximate position beforehand," Tar said.

"I know where we're at," Princess said. "But you're not going to like it."

"Well, at least somebody took the time to study the charts!" Kalleen said. "Where are we, Princess?"

"The pirate realm of Noita Zei'Chara."

Tar's jaw dropped. I groaned. Kalleen looked puzzled.

"Who is Noita Zei'Chara and where exactly is his pirate realm?"

"You don't know who he is?" Tar said as he spun around in his seat. "Where have you been for the last thirty years?!"

"What year is it?"

"3028 MWGS, uh Milky Way Galactic Standard." I answered. "When were you last activated?"

"3002 MWGS." Kalleen said. "Oedipus and his son were just beginning to build The Bloated Namreg, only the code name, of course. They had a fine name for it, but wouldn't reveal it to anyone. Has it really been twenty-six years?"

"Wait! Wait! WAIT!" Tar screamed. "Code name? Why did my ship have a code name?"

"Because of all the advanced systems built into it, like the Ultra-Drive engines, the Vortex weapons, and the transporter."

Tar stared at Kalleen. I stared at Tar. Princess stared at the stars.

"Is the Ultra-Drive responsible for sending us to the other side of the galaxy this fast?" Princess said.

"No, no. The Ultra-Drive would take a year or so to span the galaxy. It's fast, but not that fast. You probably hit a Trans-Warp." Kalleen smiled. We began asking questions all at once. It took Kalleen several minutes to calm us down.

"Now, Tar, since it is your ship, I'll answer your questions first."

"This shouldn't take too long. All of those nifty little systems that you rattled off a few minutes ago are not on my ship. 'Nuff said?" Tar smiled.

"Of course they're on your ship, Tar. You just haven't been told about them because you're not ready yet." Kalleen smiled like a maternal grandmother.

"Kalleen, I think you're missing a few pieces of this puzzle," Tar said. "First, Grandpa spent the last twenty-three years in cryogenic hibernation, not exactly able to decide whether or not I'm ready yet. Second, Dad came down with acute amnesia fifteen years ago and hasn't been even close to the same since. Since those are the only two people who could have told me if I was ready or not, how can you assume I'm not?"

"Thadius could have revealed this information to you, correct?" Kalleen smiled.

"As I've come to understand it, Thadius has not exactly been himself for the last thirteen years either."

Tar flashed a big, toothy grin, believing, as he always did, that he outsmarted a superior mind. As usual, he was wrong.

"Tar," Kalleen said. "I believe I'm a competent authority to judge whether or not you're ready for that information. From what I've seen of your behavior and demeanor so far, I wouldn't trust you with a water pistol much less the modern weaponry that is available aboard the Namreg. If you exhibited a bit more maturity now and then, I might be inclined to change that judgment," she turned to me, leaving Tar staring at the side of her head. "Now then, Gorth, I believe you had the next question."

"No, I'm fine. Thanks anyway." I tried to keep from applauding the way she just shot down Tar. I thought he needed a good tongue-lashing; however, being his best friend, I can't do it and nobody else cared enough about Tar to bother.

"Very well, then. Princess, do you have any questions for me?" Kalleen smiled at her.

"How much firepower does this ship have right now?" Princess asked.

"Well, I can only operate the precision military lasers on the forward bow. The Golden Sabre relies more on its speed than it does on firepower."

"Just how fast is The Golden Sabre?"

"It is very maneuverable at High Impulse, but it can handle simple straight-aways at Medium Hyperlight. The ship isn't big enough to handle faster speeds, besides the fact that the engine can't deliver much more thrust anyway."

I stared in shock at Kalleen. Tar turned red with anger. The Namreg could barely edge into sub-Hyperlight. I knew the information withheld from us could reveal the Namreg could reach High Hyperlight.

The structure of the Namreg could take it, but no engine I knew of could put out that kind of thrust. If the Namreg had Ultra-Drive engines, that would make it the fastest ship in existence. If the firepower secretly aboard the Namreg matched its secret speed, I understood the need to keep the information well-guarded. I agreed that Tar wasn't mature enough yet.

Princess paused to let the information sink in and started to count on her fingers. "I think the best course of action would be to turn fifteen degrees starboard and make your best speed straight ahead. We are deep inside Zei'Chara's territory. That would take us out of here the fastest."

"Good enough. Everybody hold onto your seats!" Kalleen said. The ship's maneuvering thrusters came to life and gently turned the ship starboard 15 degrees while the engines warmed up. "This is going to be a little bumpy at the start, so hang on."

The Golden Sabre's engines fired up and the ship shot forward with safety just a heartbeat away.

CHAPTER 16
FEELING FLUSHED

Bumpy didn't begin to describe the ride we experienced. One rule often observed when aboard a space vehicle is to let the engines properly warm up before going full speed ahead, especially when said engines haven't run for a while. These particular engines had been asleep for a very long time; thus, they suffered from a bit of 'crankiness.'

We were pinned against the back wall when the ship came to an abrupt halt. We hadn't buckled in very well. Tar, Princess and I peeled ourselves off the rear wall of the bridge. Several impolite adjectives flowed freely out of Tar's mouth, blood flowed freely out of my nose, and select parts of Princess' charm flowed freely out of her jumpsuit, now torn in a haphazard and unbecoming fashion.

"—elluva lot more engine to this thing so you have to let it warm up longer! In all my... I never... If there's one thing I can't... *Aaaaahhhh*! Where's my knee?!

Oh, there it is!" Tar got to his feet. "Would you please tell me who taught you... who programmed you to pilot this ship?!"

"Lady and Gentlemen, it seems that we have visitors," Kalleen said.

Several points of light moved on the bridge's screen. Everyone aboard the bridge saw the lights. Tar and I frowned, Princess had a curiously blank look on her face, and Kalleen examined the screen.

"There are seventeen ships in front of us and twenty-two to our aft. The sensors are picking up movement to our port and starboard sides, as well as above and below us. The sensors are not tuned well enough to tell how many there are, however."

Tar put his hands on his face.

"We're dead."

I just held my nose and shook my head slowly.

"No," Kalleen said. "Our weaponry can take them."

Princess watched the ships get closer. Her eyes darted around as she waited for the ships to get within range. Tar and I hopped back into our seats, strapped ourselves in, and watched the screen. Princess maneuvered somewhere in the background. As my attention was primarily focused on the screen, I didn't notice her activities.

"Five seconds until they're within range," Kalleen looked behind her. "Princess, dear, you really should get in your seat and strap yourself in, it's going to get a little bumpy for a while." Kalleen turned back towards the main screen. "Okay, folks, it's show time!"

A loud clang reverberated through the bridge, immediately followed by a hissing sound. Tar and I turned around in our seats to see Kalleen slumped on the floor. Princess covered her with foam shooting out of the slightly-dented fire extinguisher in her hands.

We struggled to get out of our seats. Princess dropped the fire extinguisher and ran to the communications console. She pulled a small device out of her ear and inserted it into the console's external interface. The picture on the main screen changed. An ominous figure appeared on the screen dressed in red and black. He had piercing black eyes and a full beard adorned with jewelry.

"Attention crew of The Golden Sabre. Your ship is in a tractor beam and you cannot escape. Any resistance on your part will result in your death. Hello, my love. It's nice to have you back."

"It's nice to be back, dearest." Princess smiled at the figure on the screen.

I watched Kalleen attempt to pierce the foam with her laser lights. The foam glowed red in several places without breaking through the foam. She gave up.

The Golden Sabre shuddered briefly as Zei'Chara's flagship reeled it into a landing bay. The hatch opened and five rather large soldiers ran in, weapons ready. Tar and I put our hands in the air as Princess walked by the soldiers. She stopped at the hatch and turned around.

"Put them in chains and put the android in an opaque sack; make sure the android doesn't get loose or the King will have your heads." She stepped off the ship leaving us to our imprisonment.

"I'd just like to hit her once... Just once, really hard!" Tar said. I grunted in agreement.

Three of the soldiers moved towards Kalleen. The other two adjusted their weapons and shot us with a bright white light. We lived in darkness and slumber for an undetermined period after that.

I awoke with a start. My head pounded like a forty

piece orchestra reaching the crescendo of the William Tell Overture. Harsh white light assaulted my eyes when I opened them. When my eyes adjusted to the light, I examined my surroundings. Metal cuffs bound me to a smooth, stone wall. Tar shared the same bonds three feet to my right shaking the cobwebs from his head. We stood in an obsidian room twenty feet long and fifteen feet wide with two doors at either end.

"Welcome back to the world of the living," I said.

Tar turned his head to me and smiled. "With the way my life has been going lately, I might be better off dead. You'd think I'd been drinking heavily considering how much of the last few weeks I've spent unconscious. How's your nose, by the way?"

"Great! I don't know how it managed to heal so well on its own."

"We operated on you, that's how," a voice stated from the east entrance to the room. Noita Zei'Chara, the pirate king, walked into the room. He wore a regal red and black outfit trimmed in gold. He even wore a crown. Princess and two guards followed close behind. Princess wore a beautiful red and black silk dress that showed very nearly every curve of her body. She displayed a small amount of make-up on her face with a grace that surprised me. We both gulped in astonishment when we saw her. Somehow, she managed to transcend attractive and was downright beautiful. The guards wore matching red and black uniforms, but carried no weaponry. "I like to have my guests in good health before I offer them a position in my organization."

The tall king walked in front of Tar and smiled.

"Tar Reztap. I knew your grandfather, but I won't hold that against you. Your reputation as a troublemaker precedes you—I can always use someone like that on my front line." He walked in front of me. "And Gorth, I hear you are quite the handyman around Tar's ship. We can always use talented technicians around here. I want to thank you for rescuing my prize concubine. Isn't she beautiful." He reached out and caressed Princess' golden tresses. The two guards leered. "So, I'll offer you two a choice. You can join my organization or you can... leave."

"What about The Golden Sabre?" Tar asked.

"Oh, you can have it the moment you walk into the hangar it's stored in," Zei'Chara said smiling pleasantly at us. "Even if you choose to leave."

Tar and I looked at each other.

"We'll leave!" we said in unison.

"Oh, I'm sorry to hear that. But, I am a man of my word," Zei'Chara said as he snapped his fingers. One of the guards pressed a button next to the door. The wall that held us rotated until we hung face down approximately four feet off the floor. The floor below us folded away, revealing a wide steel ramp leading to what looked like a cliff. Sewer sludge poured out of a pipe just above the wall, leaving a thick putrid coat on the surface.

"And remember," Zei'Chara said. "You can have your ship when you walk into the hangar."

The metal cuffs holding us to the wall clicked open. We fell onto the ramp and slid off the edge. We hit a slope and slid down several hundred feet through sludge before we slowed down and reached the bottom. The gap we fell from closed, cutting us off from the obsidian room above.

At this time, the smell really hit us hard. I puked until I dry heaved, tears streaming down my face. Tar started with projectile vomiting until he too had nothing left in his stomach. We wretched so hard our sides and heads ached, and then we wretched some more. Time passed, probably only minutes, but it seemed like forever before we got accustomed to the horrendous stench surrounding us.

I got up and started to brush the sludge off. I didn't get very far before stopping the pointless activity. I sat back down in the sludge. Tar just laid in it for a while.

"My life has come to this, being flushed down a toilet," Tar said and sat up. "So, it can't possibly get worse. I mean, I've lost my ship, mom's red scarf, grandpa, had grandpa's ship taken by pirates, had my android melt before my eyes, been kicked in the crotch and seen naked by Zei'Chara's lover, and flushed down the proverbial toilet into a sewer dungeon. From this perspective, things can only get better."

Tar stood up and started walking. He stopped and turned around to look at me.

"Well, are you coming or what?"

I grunted in annoyance, stood up and followed Tar.

"She saw you naked?"

"It was unintentional. Nothing happened. Get your mind out the sewer."

Zei'Chara's home planet, Orridon, was a lush and beautiful class G-5 planet. Barrooms across the galaxy chatted up the white sandy beaches, immense forests and breathtaking vistas covering the sparsely populated orb. The capital city, Teltosh, combined modern design with amazing architectural masterpieces lining every street. By all standards, the best that ill-gotten booty can buy. In recent years, Orridon flourished as a major trading center for this part of the galaxy. The wealth flowing in from this trade dwarfed the pirating income, transforming this lush outpost into the ruling kingdom of several solar systems. Beneath this teeming mecca laid the sewers.

The mostly underground dungeon comprised much of the planet's sewer system. Above ground entrances allowed the introduction of a variety of deadly creatures, as well as standard sewer sludge into the dungeon. Decades of rumors hold that no one ever escaped the pirate king's dungeon, or lived to tell the tale if they had. Based on the number of people that disappeared every year traversing this sector of space, common wisdom dictated several dozen humanoids, aliens, and creatures lived and survived in the dungeons.

As fresh faces in the neighborhood, it seemed proper we would meet one of them.

CHAPTER 17
WORM FOOD

We trudged through the dungeon for several hours before stopping to rest. I searched for somewhere decent to sit. After a ten minute search, I finally located a clean looking pipe about five feet off the floor of the dungeon. I carefully hopped up onto the pipe, promptly slid off the super-slick surface, and landed in the sludge. I lay there and pouted. Tar took this as a sign to take a rest himself and sat down. The object Tar sat down on collapsed leaving him sitting in waist deep sludge.

"It just has to get better, Gorth. It has to."

A few minutes passed before we heard a loud growly gurgle, which brought both of us to our feet. We stood silently, not daring to breath. Several seconds passed before the source of the sound revealed itself. A large, scaly worm rose up from the muck and towered over us.

"Its events just like this which defeat optimism, Gorth," Tar said as he dodged the worm's first attack, a headlong dive at its prey. Tar looked around for something to fight the beast off with; he saw sludge.

The beast rose up again and swung towards me with surprising speed. Blue and green teeth grew large in my eyes, the remains of the beast's last victim still evident on the fangs. I didn't even have time to think, so I let instinct take over. Instinct looked at what it was facing and knew a bad thing when it saw one, so it let improvisation take over. Improvisation jury-rigged a little aid from dumb luck, and I threw a powerhouse punch at the worm's lower jaw. This action had several effects; it stunned the worm, surprised Tar, saved my life, broke my right hand and, upon smelling the creature's breath at such a close range, rendered me unconscious. Decayed Fredowurg guts tend to have that effect on a person when sniffed at close range.

The worm lay next to me, rapidly blinking its beady, black eyes. My own eyes struggled to focus as I saw its huge head rock left and right. I assumed the worm attempted to stop the world from spinning. Tar rapped a nearly clean bandana around his mouth and nose. He drug me away from the dazed worm. I struggled back to full consciousness, but couldn't move just yet. Now that he had a minute or two, Tar searched through the muck for something to slay the beast with. Unfortunately, he couldn't find anything but a twenty-foot length of steel cord.

"Well," he said. "If I can't kill the thing, I might as well slow it up. Might even keep it from killing us." He took the cord, walked over to the still dazed worm, and wrapped the cord around its jaws, tying them securely shut. He carefully threaded the cord through the nostrils before tying it off to keep the slimy monstrosity from trying to get loose too soon. When he finished, Tar returned to me and examined my hand. Not a mess, but definitely broken. Tar grabbed a couple chunks of ceramic tile that floating on top of the sludge behind him. Not very sturdy but good enough, Tar used the tile and our bandanas to temporarily splint my broken hand.

Tar knelt next to me.

"My hand hurts."

"You broke it."

"Oh. Where's the worm?"

"Alive, but stunned, about ten feet to your left... well... not stunned anymore."

The worm stirred. It shook its head a few times and then reared up above us, glaring at me with hatred.

"I tied its-" Tar began to say, but stopped himself as the worm opened its jaws, quickly and easily snapping the cord wrapped around its jaw. Both frayed ends of the cord hung loosely from its nostrils. It stopped for a moment, trying to see what dangled from its nose. It shook its head again, and let out a horrendous, high-pitched screech. We both got to our feet. I started to run, but Tar grabbed my arm.

"What are you doing?!"

"When the worm dives at us, grab the frayed end of that cord," Tar said.

"Are you nuts?"

"Trust me."

I got a sick feeling in my stomach whenever Tar said those two words.

"If you get me killed, I'm going to haunt you mercilessly."

The worm zeroed in on us, opened its jaws hungrily, and dove. We stood our ground, waiting for the right moment. When we detected the stench of the worm's last meal, we leaped at the worm and succeeded in grabbing the ends of the cord. The worm stopped abruptly and reared its head, leaving us dangling a few feet off the ground.

"You see," Tar shouted to me hanging from the other end of the cord, "the cord is causing it pain as well as preventing it from closing its nostrils and traveling below the sludge."

"Well, Tar," I said, as I held onto the cord with my one good hand, "you're smarter than I gave you credit for."

Just then the beast shook its head violently, attempting to dislodge us. Failing in that attempt, it tried to snap at us with its jaws. We were just out of reach. It shook its head again.

"I don't think this is hurting it, Tar!"

"Well, it still can't-" The worm cut off Tar's shout by closing its nostrils around the cord and diving into the sludge, taking us along for the ride.

Twenty seconds later, the worm surfaced in an entirely different part of the underground dungeon. We dangled precariously from our respective ends of the steel cord threaded through the beast's nostrils and gasped for breath.

"Tar, I swear-" I said before the beast dived back towards the grimy surface.

"So do I," Tar added before taking his breath.

Once again, we experienced sludge.

The next time the worm resurfaced, we felt the need to call it quits. To our surprise, however, it didn't go under a third time primarily because six crossbow bolts suddenly appeared in the thing's head. The beast dropped to the ground. We lay beside it, exhausted.

"Hmmph. It's no wonder tha beastie almost got ya if'n ye're dumb enough to lie around tha sewer like tha."

We looked up at the source of the voice talking to

us. It belonged to a rather tall Fredowurg. The alien with canine features and black fur raised its eyebrows.

"You Fredowurgs look much better when you're not partially digested," I said.

"Thank ya... I think. Name's Dilo Pizwix," Dilo said as he retrieved his bolts from the worm's head and examined them for damage. He licked the blue worm blood off the bolts and placed them back in his quiver.

"Well, thank YOU, Dilo!" Tar said as he jumped up out of the muck. "I'm Tar and this is Gorth. You just saved our lives, for which we're quite thankful!"

"Oh, tha. Don' be too thankful; I dinna do it fer ya, I did it fer me. Canna 'ave sewer worms that like tha taste of Fredowurgs running loose now can I? One o' our best defenses against predators is tha we dinna taste very good. In fact, we taste downright awful," Dilo got a dreamy look in his eye. "Heck, tha only good thing tha came of it was tha stupid thing ate me mum."

"It ate your mother?" I said looking at the dead beast lying a few feet away as it slowly sunk into the muck.

"Yep, it sure did." Dilo scratched himself behind the right ear.

"And you're happy about this?" Tar said.

"Look, how would ya feel if ya'd spent tha last seven years down 'ere in this stink hole wit yer mum?"

We looked at each other in discomfort. I had to admit the idea was less than pleasant.

"Well," Tar said, "if it doesn't bother you, I guess it doesn't bother us."

"Good. Not tha I really care what either o' ya think, but it's nice to know I dinna have hostile enemies runnin' about pissed a' me 'cause I don't miss me mum," Dilo smiled briefly, then turned around and began to walk away. We followed.

An hour passed before Dilo came to a halt with us a few paces behind him. We stopped when he held up his hand briefly, signaling us to stop. The hair on the back of his neck stood on end. He pulled out a bolt from the quarrel on his back, loaded his crossbow, and carefully aimed at the floor near a pipe to his left. I looked where he aimed and barely detected a thin column of steam shooting up from the floor. Dilo fired. A small, scaly monster about the size of Tar's head leaped out from under the muck, a crossbow bolt protruding from its single breathing hole. The little beast looked like nothing but one huge mouth full of teeth. It scurried off down the pipe away from us, screeching the entire way.

"Nasty lil bugger. Kill ya in three seconds flat, if it gets its teeth inna ya," Dilo said as he walked into the pipe. "Lucky for us it dint know ya can see it breathin. All mouth and no brain... kinda like me mum."

Dilo stopped under a hole in the pipe. He reached up, grabbed the bottom rung of a concealed ladder, and climbed up. We watched in curious silence. A brief click sounded from the hole, followed by a barely audible squeaking.

"Okay, come on up," Dilo yelled down. Tar helped me up the ladder and followed.

We emerged into a small cavity carved out of the cement and earth. It held several beds, as well as a few items of furniture, that could easily accommodate a dozen occupants. The one feature of the dwellings that most intrigued us was the sound of falling water.

"Say, Dilo," I said, "that sound wouldn't per chance be a shower, would it?"

"Uh, what?" Dilo looked up from fiddling with his

crossbow. "Shower? Well, ya, guess ya could call it that. Hang on 'n' I'll give ya tha grand tour." Dilo set his weapon down on a table, careful to not leave it loaded. He paused, staring intently at the wall next to the table. With a swift swipe of his arm, he snatched up a crawling bug and popped it in his mouth. It took two bites for him to down the bug due to its large size. Tar and I watched in silence. Being well traveled and knowledgeable, I knew that Fredowurgs loved the taste of fresh insects, and barely acknowledged the action. Tar put his hand to his mouth and closed his eyes, but remained silent.

"This," Dilo said as he walked down the wall to his left and stopped at the first doorway. "...is tha kitchen area. Ya clean off any surface to tha best of yer ability afore preparin' yer food on it. All sorts of different cultures represented 'ere... some of 'em actually cook thar food. *Blech!*" Dilo shuddered for a moment. "Ya eat what ya kill, ya prepare what ya kill. If ya don't kill nuttin, ya don't eat, and ya die. Got it?"

We nodded. Dilo continued to the next doorway. I glimpsed briefly into the kitchen and immediately wished I hadn't. A Wifflit cyborg eagerly consumed a freshly slaughtered Senuvian Drot. I groaned and returned my attention to our host.

"This is the 'shower,' as ya call it. Requires two biped humanoids, or tha equivalent, ta start it 'n' shut it off. Ichtin managed ta tap a water main for this convenience. Ya gotta be considerit 'n' shut it off afta ya use it, so's the `leakage' innit noticed. Been lucky so far; although, thar was a month we went wiffout. Thought our lil abode'd be discovered. They sent workers down tha pipe lookin' for tha leak. Ichtin had tha' covered. His lil invention's undetectable from inside tha pipe."

A loud noise interrupted the tour. Some of the residents had returned from a day's hunting.

"Veritable misuse of valuable chronological continuum!" one of the voices shouted.

"A waste of time," a second somewhat subdued voice followed.

"Ya ol' bag o' wind! I dinna care wha ya think, we're gonna do it anyway!" a third voice shouted back.

We left the shower room to see who was so loud. We turned a corner into a separate cavern with a hole in the center of the floor similar to the one we entered through. Gathered around the hole were three humanoids: one Huck'too, another Fredowurg, and a Blaufft. As the conversation progressed, it became evident that the Blaufft interpreted what the Huck'too said so the Fredowurg could understand it. After a while, I began to ignore the Huck'too and just listened to the Blaufft. The porcine Huck'too had an annoying habit of using big words to get their point across, usually hoping to win an argument by confusing their opponent. Sometimes they won just by being pigheaded. The feathered Blaufft were highly intelligent in some areas, language being one of them, and made the best interpreters in the known universe. Unfortunately, they weren't good for much else, but they had beautiful plumage.

"Inconsequential evidence indicates premature assumptions by the opposing viewpoint."

"You have no proof," the Blaufft said as it started preening its feathers.

"Look 'ere, ya dumb ninny, I never been surer o' anythin' in my miserable life; if we dinna do it, we're histry! Kaput! No longer o' any value ta anythin' but a meat-eater! Dead. Understand?" The Fredowurg was quite adamant about his point of view, whereas the

Huck'too seemed to be arguing specifically for the pleasure of arguing. The Blaufft seemed to be happy that he had any utility at all.

"Respectfully annotated. However, I must undertake disbelief at your qualifications to appropriately decipher all of the elements and permutations of the event in question."

"You don't know what you're talking about."

"I don't... why, I... ooooooh!" The Fredowurg growled and stormed off into the main room, brushing past us. The Huck'too and Blaufft walked up to our small group and smiled.

"Folks," Dilo said. "I'd like you to meet Graustish and his translator, Fift." We nodded at them. "These two boys are Tar 'n' Gorth, new to tha slum."

"Your acquaintance promulgates pleasant tidings in the tranquil atmosphere of this dwelling," Graustish said with a smile, twitching his snout in the customary greeting of the Huck'too.

"We're pleased to meet you," Fift translated.

"Begging your favor, ourselves must depart to carry on important business elsewhere."

"Excuse us."

Graustish and Fift smiled as they headed for the kitchen. Fift had a slimy, dead beast slung across his back, no doubt ready for roasting or whatever. I raised my eyebrows.

"Those two seem ta think they're our resident geniuses," Dilo said.

"What were they arguing about?" I said.

"I believe they were questionin' tha wisdom o' Ichtin's decision ta open Xetoch's Tomb."

"Why?" Tar said.

"Legend 'as it there's a great weapon in Xetoch's Tomb that'll free us from tha dungeon. It'd 'ave ta be great ta get us out of here 'n' fight Zei'Chara at tha same time."

"Would you mind if we came along? The name Xetoch seems familiar." Tar seemed to be concentrating hard as he said it.

"Tha more tha merrier! Frankly, I canna think o' anybody in all o' tha sewers tha won't be there."

My thoughts wandered to food and my stomach thanked me for the recognition by aching dully.

"Is there a chance we could get something to eat?"

"Certainly. Yer first meal is on tha house; but, then ye're on yer own." Dilo headed towards the kitchen. "Say, yer kind likes food cooked, doncha? Grab a shower 'n' I'll hunt up someone ta cook it fer ya. I'll pop by Benny tha cyborg 'n' see if he can do somethin' 'bout your 'and too, Gorth. E's got a bone mender built into 'is circuitry, among otha 'andy gadgets," Dilo said disappearing into the kitchen.

I immediately strode to the shower. Tar trailed lazily behind me.

CHAPTER 18
A Nice Helping of Tomb Surprise

The twenty foot square door to the tomb divided into four triangular sections forming a large 'X'. Opinion among the captives oscillated between the X signifying lost treasure or identifying the tomb's sole inhabitant. Ichtin used some etchings from the door to narrow the burial chamber age to be equivalent to the dungeon, at least twenty years old. It took three weeks and a considerable amount of construction with improvised materials to keep the ninety by twenty foot plot in front of the tomb clear of sludge.

The top three rusted sections had ropes attached to the outer edge. Each rope ran the length of the tunnel through a series of ratcheting pulleys coming out at the other end of the tunnel. Each rope had a large group of detainees waiting to pull when the signal came. The dungeon's entire complement of prisoners gathered for the opening. Graustish and Fift had graced the event with their presence merely to gloat over their prediction that nothing of any use would be discovered in the tomb.

We joined the hundred or so dungeon dwellers manning the ropes to hoist the sections of the tomb. The largest of the dungeon's inhabitants anchored each rope. I noted that my Wifflit cyborg doctor, Benny, anchored the center rope and secured himself to the ground with climbing claws protruding from his feet.

At least two guards manned each entrance to the tunnel to watch for Zei'Chara's troops. No one including Ichtin could predict how much noise this archeological excavation would make. Because of his deadly accuracy with the crossbow, Dilo guarded the entrance to the tomb itself. No one knew what the tomb contained and all of them faced some dangerous creatures at one time or another in the depths of the dungeon. Ichtin studied the set-up, double-checking everything from the attachments at the door sections to the bare ground that provided traction for the rope-pullers. Ichtin walked to the front of the tunnel and stood next to Dilo. The ominous tomb door loomed above them.

"Men," Ichtin said. He stood tall and raised his arms out to the gathered crowd. "I think it's 'bout time we opened this stinkin' door!"

Everyone chuckled.

"One... Two... *Pull*!"

The ropes strained under the task before them. Eighteen pulleys of dubious looking construction creaked and groaned under the sudden strain. Seconds passed and nothing happened. Ichtin squinted at the tomb door from where he stood.

"Let off!" Ichtin said as he walked up to examine the door. The ropes went slack and everyone on the rope crew took a breath. Ichtin looked closely at the seal between the sections, hoping for any sign of a break in the seal, but none could be detected. He sniffed it briefly. His keen sense of smell couldn't detect any change.

"Try it again," Ichtin said and strode back to his spot next to Dilo. "One... Two... *Pull!*"

Again the rope crew struggled as the pulleys creaked and groaned. After thirty seconds passed, Ichtin called another break. He examined the door for a few minutes. After a quick sniff, he turned around with a sly grin.

"I smell fresh concrete. We're makin' progress! Let's give it another go!"

The rope crew looked at each other, our mouths set in a firm, but determined scowl. We gritted our teeth, stretched our shoulders and grabbed the rope again with a tighter grip. A nervous murmur rolled like a wave through the crowd. Ichtin took a deep breath.

"One... Two... *Pulllll!*"

The ropes hummed like guitar strings being plucked. The tomb door appeared unaffected. Ten seconds passed. Ichtin frowned at the door. My muscles screamed for relief as the others around me groaned but didn't let up. A sharp sound—a metallic crack—punctured the air and echoed through the tunnels of the dungeon. The three upper sections fell to the ground in a dusty haze and a thunderous crash. A brief sigh of relief punctured the air.

Then we saw the Drots.

The battle cry rang out and everyone dropped their ropes and grabbed the nearest weapon they could find. Some swung chunks of wood, others whipped bits of cable through the air, knocking the flying jellyfish out of the air and against the concrete walls. Dilo saved his fellow prisoners more than a dozen times with a well-placed crossbow bolt. Some of the more gifted denizens engaged the Drots with natural weapons. The bearlike Ursinites clawed their way through several tentacled menaces, while amphibian humanoids used sticky appendages to grasp the enemy and drown them in the mucky waters. Benny snagged a few out of mid-air and split them open using his built in scalpels and screwdrivers. Tar and I managed to grapple one to the ground, disabling it with a swift kick to the head.

The battle raged on for several hours, a few men lost their faces to the vicious cyborg jellyfish. But no one gave up and ran. The odd bond among the subterranean captives rivaled the camaraderie prisoners of war shared. Luckily, when the battle ended we could say no one lost their lives, although with several people being suddenly faceless, we found it much harder to identify them. Senuvian Drots absorbed the fatty tissues that lay beneath the surface of the skin on the victim's face and the venom ejected into their victim deadened all of the nerve endings in the immediate and surrounding area. Benny consoled the victims and said he'd be able to help them after he consumed a significant portion of the Drot smorgasbord filling the tunnel.

Only one section of the tomb door remained in place, the bottom one made of stone. Every able bodied person grabbed the edge of this section and pulled. This did nothing. We tried climbing over it, only to discover that the final section blocked off an entirely separate chamber from the Drot nest.

Anger at the sudden impasse spread like wildfire. Even the people attacked by the Drots who couldn't keep their eyes open or speak because of their deadened facial muscles grunted in protest. I admit to feeling a bit crestfallen myself.

Ichtin stood fast, tuning out the angry voices, and thought for a moment on how to remove the last section of the tomb door. He examined the edges, touching and sniffing every exposed inch of stone. Two indented slots where the two side sections had joined it offered nothing in the way of clues. The section appeared to be much thicker than the other three sections, which made it heavier but shouldn't stop the brute force exerted by the masses in the tunnels from budging it. He climbed up into the Senuvian Drot nest and examined it, looking for a hidden entrance or switch.

While Ichtin studied the nest and everyone else yelled at him, Tar walked up to the last remaining section and leaned on it. The last section began to sink into the chamber behind it. Tar spun around, but otherwise didn't move except to flick the safety off on his crossbow. Ichtin jumped out of the nest and the others just stood back, keeping their guard up. Tar stood silent in front of them all. Sweat trickled from my brow down my nose and I swiped at it with the back of my hand. My friend faced the unknown with a thick wall of fellow dungeon dwellers separating me from him. If anything sudden and catastrophic happened, I could do nothing to help him.

The final section continued to move away from Tar until it became flush with the wall behind, and then the entire wall dropped into the ground. Bright light erupted from the inner chamber of the tomb. Everyone shielded their eyes. A musty cloud of dust erupted from the new opening, briefly engulfing Tar. When the dust cleared, the waning light revealed a long, tubular machine sitting in the center of the chamber. Tar smiled and ran into the chamber.

"Ichtin, get in here quick!"

Ichtin rushed to Tar's side at the machine. He ran his hands over the smooth metal surface. He sniffed the dials and looked underneath at the multiple pipes and tubes running into the floor and the surrounding walls.

"Oh my. A generational cryogeni' tube. I ne'er thought I'd actually see one." Ichtin's eyes glazed over and he shook his head. He put his paws over his mouth a made a small "yip".

"Do you think you can operate it?" Tar asked. I recalled Thadius had deactivated Oedipus' long term cryogenic chamber. Neither Tar nor I had any idea how to work one.

"How 'bout this switch marked 'Awaken'?" Ichtin looked up at Tar and smiled.

Tar frowned. He looked out the entrance to the chamber and saw everyone assembled and watching. He set his shoulders and flicked the switch.

The machine hissed like a giant snake. The metal tube began to separate down the center. Tar and Ichtin stepped back as a fine mist billowed forth and the machine hummed softly. A hush fell over the crowd in the chamber. A few seconds passed before we could see the person encased in the machine. The cryogenic tube inhabitant blinked rapidly, but sat up slowly. He stared at the group gathered around him. The humanoid had an orange-grey hue to his skin and fiery red hair slightly grey at the temples. He yawned, revealing a set of sharp, carnivorous teeth.

"A blanket would be handy, right about now."

"Xetoch," Tar said. "My grandfather, Oedipus Reztap, sends his greetings."

Someone found a blanket and handed it to Xetoch, who was staring at Tar. His eyes got wide.

"Looks like I've been away for quite a while," Xetoch said glancing at the control panel on the cryotube. "That old codger's still alive?"

"Alive and well," Tar said. "He doesn't look a day over 48."

"Incredible! He should be in his 70's by now... unless..." Xetoch shook his head. "Of course, Thadius must have gotten bored and designed a generational cryotube for himself as well. Looks like our partying days aren't over yet!"

Xetoch jumped out of the cryotube and promptly fell flat on his face.

"Thadius probably built him a better model than my makeshift body-freezer." Xetoch sat up and grabbed onto the side of the cryotube. He shook his head.

Tar and I helped Xetoch to his feet. He looked at his hand and then out at everyone else standing around. "Hope I'll get to see color again."

A few people in the crowd started mumbling. A few pushed each other and I think I heard one of the amphibians croak.

"Hey, Ichtin!" a small, but sturdy Gretn'aak shouted, waving all four of his arms. "Where's this great weapon that's supposed to be here?!"

The crowd started to grumble. One without a face tried valiantly to grumble. Unfortunately, it came out as more of a whimper, at which point he cried. His deadened face muscles couldn't control their eyelids, which simply bulged until the pressure increased enough for the liquid to seep out.

"Fellow prisoners! It is I, Xetoch, the first prisoner of Zei'Chara's dungeon who is your greatest weapon of all... I know how to get out!"

A hush fell over the room. A feeling of joy and excitement electrified the air.

"By the way," Xetoch continued in a hopeful tone, "would any of you happen to have an atomic bomb lying about the dungeon that you're not using?"

CHAPTER 19
THE UNINSPIRED LEADING THE CLUELESS

Xetoch ate ravenously like a man who hadn't eaten for weeks. He sat in the main dwelling chamber with me, Tar, Dilo, Ichtin, Graustish, and Fift. We gaped at the display of Xetoch's voracious appetite; Graustish, in particular, looked a bit green around the ear flaps.

"Whew!" Xetoch exclaimed as he finished downing the remains of a boiled sewer worm. "Before I got into that cryotube, I hadn't eaten for weeks." He gulped down a swig of purified water. "Nothing substantial, anyway. Being the first inhabitant of the dungeons, I discovered the belt tightening scarcity of food–the primary reason I started building the cryotube in the first place.

"The only food I could find consisted primarily of the remains of meals the workers left half-eaten before they sealed off the dungeons. Those fairly edible finds lasted until about the third day of my incarceration; by then, everything else I found had turned pretty green. Luckily, they hadn't started dumping any sewage into the place yet. I don't think they finished connecting all the pipes up above until after I encapsulated myself like a frozen corpse." Xetoch paused to scoop up the last bit of worm entrails and then sat back in his chair.

"Interesting days, my friends. Scavenging all of the building materials and tools left behind by the workers. You know, now that I think about it, probably a damn good thing I got Zei'Chara so riled at me. If he hadn't been so angry, he wouldn't have rushed completion of the dungeons just so he could throw me into them. The workers forgot about clean-up and concentrated on finishing construction. I had all the materials I needed, except for one thing: energy.

"It turned out to be my biggest dilemma, and I had to solve it before I could begin building the cryotube. I wound up tracing the work lights to a central point in the dungeon. They all came to the wall just outside where you found me. I knew where the workers had last been in the dungeon; at that sealed up wall. Over the first days of scrounging for food, I came across a cement drill and a generator among other handy tools. I had the tools to escape the dungeons with; however, I knew Zei'Chara too. He wouldn't leave potential exit points unguarded. What's more, how could I leave the planet once I escaped the dungeon?" Xetoch stood up and walked around the room as he talked.

"Well, I did leave the dungeon, so to speak, once or twice. I burrowed through the ground until I came to the anchoring pylons of a power relay station. Then I burrowed up to the basement of the station and tapped into one of the back-up generators that always ran. The amount of energy I tapped out would go unnoticed and be very untraceable. Then, I sealed myself back into the dungeon."

Dilo started at this. "Wait a minute! You dinna try ta find food while ya were out? Why not?"

"Because, my short and very mean looking friend, I didn't want to increase the chances of my getting caught. If I got caught, you can bet Zei'Chara would discover my little life preservation project and take it all away, personally ensuring that the dungeons remained too clean for me to do a thing. If Zei'Chara ever had an inkling of my activities down here..." Xetoch shuddered.

"Just the same, I knew he'd check up on me. So I developed a quick-drying, biodegradable cement that once covered the four sections of the entrance to my 'tomb.' I believe it lasted about five years before it broke down chemically; maybe sooner, depending on the chemicals contained in the sewage they piped in here. But, I digress.

"I finally built the machine, liberating a few spare parts from the basement of that power relay station, and put myself in cryogenic hibernation. I designed the machine to start generating its own power with the generator and begin a wake up sequence if they cut the power lines from the relay station. Really, I executed a simple plan from conception to inception when you think about it."

The room was silent. Graustish wiggled his snout and spoke.

"Would someone be so kind as to relay the identity of the individual responsible for requesting a lengthy narration of the fellow incarcerate's history?"

Before Fift could translate, Xetoch immediately replied.

"Sorry, laddie. Just passing time while my food

digested, as well as planning our defense against Zei'Chara's imminent attack," Xetoch said, stood up and began to walk to the exit hole.

"Attack?" Tar squeaked.

"Surely our fellow incarcerate exaggerates the immediacy of our preparations."

"We have plenty of time, right?" Fift translated.

Xetoch turned and smiled.

"Certainly! I figure we have a full two hours before he swarms this place. Of course, if he's grown lazy, it might be two and a half; but I wouldn't count on it," Xetoch said and climbed down the ladder.

All of us stood there staring at the exit hole. Tar's mouth hung open at a curious angle. I frowned. Dilo screwed up his face into a nasty frown; then retrieved his crossbow and started down the ladder after Xetoch. Graustish sat down and scratched his head, for which Fift provided no translation. Tar shook his head and ran to the hole.

"Xetoch! Care to clue us in on how you know this?" Tar yelled down as he climbed.

The rest of us finally moved and followed Tar.

"Good citizens of the dungeons!" Xetoch shouted at the gathered crowd thirty minutes after leaving the main dwelling. "In a short while, the troops of Noita Zei'Chara will storm this place... probably with gas masks on."

Everyone chuckled.

"You all must gather up your weapons and spare provisions and meet me back here in twenty minutes. Then, I'll give you our battle plans." Xetoch turned to Tar and I standing behind him looking lost. "That means you too."

"Yeah, yeah," I said as Tar and I turned to go. "Quick like a bunny rabbit."

"Quick like a what?" Tar said trudging along behind me.

When the full complement of dungeon dwellers returned, Xetoch stood before them with four thick boards about three feet long, a hammer, a bag of nails, and two shovels.

"Men, here is our battle plan... we're getting the hell out of here before Zei'Chara gets here." Xetoch marched to the wall to his left, pulling Tar and Dilo along. My recuperating hand prevented me from aiding in the capacity that Xetoch had in mind.

"After carefully measuring the natural body of water down here, I determined these boards are exactly one inch wider than the sludge is deep," Xetoch said as he handed the boards to Tar and the hammer and nails to Dilo. "Nail these together like this," Xetoch put his hands in a square configuration. "Use only two nails for each side. Put it down against the wall here." He pointed to a spot right next to him. "And hold it tight against the wall. Quickly now!"

Tar and Dilo went to work. By the time Xetoch had picked out two shovelers, Dilo hammered in the last nail. It took nearly fifteen minutes to clear the floor of the tunnel within the wooden frame using shovels. As the sludge cleared, two sunken handles in the floor were revealed. When there wasn't enough sludge to bother with anymore, the two men stopped shoveling.

"Dilo, if you'd be so kind as to help me with this," Xetoch said, pointing to the handles. Dilo helped him lift the newly revealed trap door. It sealed off the passageway underneath, preventing it from being filled with sludge. A nine-foot square hole opened to the passageway down below. They lugged the thick cement slab several feet away from the opening and dropped it into the sludge, where it quickly disappeared. Xetoch stood up and looked at the crowd before him.

"Single file everybody, quickly but carefully."

The whole process took almost thirty minutes. Xetoch directed, glancing every couple of seconds in either direction.

"Don't dally. My predictions could always be a bit off and time is getting short," he said as one of the dungeon denizens paused to scrape off his boots before climbing into the hole.

Others took over Tar and Dilo holding duties halfway through the evacuation, but they remained behind with me to help the odder shaped inhabitants squeeze through the passage. Finally, we lowered Xetoch through the opening. Suddenly, a loud scraping noise echoed throughout the tunnels and excited voices and shouts rose up in the distance, bouncing off the sewer walls.

"Xetoch," I said in a loud whisper. "You go ahead! We'll hold them off as long as we can!"

Tar gave me an exasperated look. "Are you that brave or that bullheaded? I can never keep the two straight."

"Trust me," Xetoch replied from beneath them. "It's all been taken care of, assuming you three can get down here in the next forty-five seconds."

We moved like there was fire lit under our feet. Xetoch handed me a shovel and quickly instructed me to bring it down with all my might on the jointed areas that held the boards together in their temporary square shape. Even with my afflicted hand, no one else in range of the hole could perform this duty any better. In one swift motion, I hacked into the first connection and then the second. The sludge flowed forward and I ducked quickly. Xetoch slid another slab of cement that had been adjacent to the trap door, but beneath the wall of the tunnel above, into place. It provided a neat seal. Somewhere above our heads, I imagined the sludge flowed over the boards, effectively blocking them from view. Xetoch turned to Tar and smiled.

"Now what?" Xetoch asked.

"Why are you looking at me?" Tar actually turned around in the narrow tunnel to see if Xetoch had someone else in mind.

"Because, Tar Reztap, your grandfather wouldn't have sent you after me if he didn't know you could get us out of here," Xetoch said and continued smiling that annoying smile I recognized instantly as the one people wear when they know something you don't and are just tickled to death about it. Tar grimaced.

"This is like that test I studied three days for, only to draw a complete blank when the page with the numbered questions appeared on the desk screen in front of me. Could you possibly elaborate in easy to understand words?"

"I traveled with Oedipus before your father's birth until shortly before your birth, I would estimate. I know your grandfather as well as he knows me. I can plan the best get-away in the world, given enough time and enough information. I knew exactly what it would take to get out of the dungeons; unfortunately, it would take plenty of men and a good deal of quick thinking to get further than the planet's surface. I can plan with the best of them, but I choke when it comes to quick thinking. That's why your grandfather sent you. You can think quickly in a desperate situation, just as he would. No matter how erratic it might be, whatever you come up with will most likely be the one thing that no one else including the enemy had thought of. Oedipus sent you to get me or rather us out."

Tar looked at me, then back at Xetoch.

"When we get out of here, I'm going to need some serious headache medication."

Several hours later, the group arrived at the place closest to where Tar and I, as well as most of the group, had entered the dungeon. When we told him of the location, Xetoch quickly derived that it was the main drainage point for Zei'Chara's palace; he knew this labyrinth of forgotten access ways and makeshift tunnels better than most people knew their hometown and led us directly to the spot described.

"Do any of you know how to get to the main space hangar from the palace?" Tar asked.

One of the three Telshi present stepped forward. The Telshi had chameleon like skin that shifted while you looked at them. They stood five foot tall and had hair that looked like leaves. I imagined they blended into their native forest landscape incredibly well.

"Do you guarantee to provide transportation for all of us from this planet?" it asked.

Tar looked behind the Telshi at the group gathered behind it. Just over a hundred assorted beings in total stared back at him. He smiled.

"Well, I can't guarantee that it will be too comfortable, but I can get you all out of here, yes."

"The hangar you are looking for is 1000 feet north of the palace's main entrance," the Telshi said and stepped back into the crowd. I then lost sight of the Telshi—he simply vanished.

"Xetoch?"

Xetoch smiled and led the way.

It took another fifteen minutes to wind our way through the labyrinth of tunnels to reach the specified spot. Xetoch located one of the hatches leading into the building above and cracked it open. He expected the total darkness he saw on the other side of the hatch.

The abandoned basement under the hangar mirrored all the other basements he encountered when he first explored the tunnels. He went ahead to check everything out and then returned. Everyone could pile out into the basement in relative safety. Tar and I became the scouting party; no one else knew what The Golden Sabre looked like besides Xetoch, and he opted to stay behind to keep the group in line.

The pirate king had opted to keep The Golden Sabre in a separate hangar all by itself; it looked like some kind of processing and testing facility. Various large machines dotted the walls connected by wires and tubes leading into the ship. I examined the machines surrounding us, while Tar checked out the ship. The ship was suspended in mid-air by a small anti-gravity device attached to her belly allowing it to be seen from all sides. From a quick inspection, Tar determined the ship had no damage and could operate with no foreseeable issues.

"We can't get inside, but I'm not concerned. The only way the researchers could get the ship running is to completely redo the interior and controls or somehow get Kalleen to cooperate with them. My first impression of Kalleen affirms the unlikelihood of that ever happening," Tar said.

I discovered a concealed door during my examination of the machines and readouts. I motioned Tar to my side and we slowly pried it open. Inside the room lay a clean, polished and inert Kalleen. Outside of the ship, her android body apparently ceased to function.

"Maybe this is your grandfather's way of keeping some degree of control over Kalleen; she has quite a strong and domineering personality."

"I can see the utility of that design," Tar said.

"Then again, perhaps the only way to supply enough energy to her at the time of her manufacture involved a direct link to the ship's power systems. Hopefully, all we have to do is get her aboard the ship," I said.

"I still like the design."

We removed all of the wires and various attachments from Kalleen's body; then I attempted to lift her. Aside from my bad hand, the weight of her metallic body prevented me from lifting her all by myself. Tar helped, but to no avail. Her resilience could be due to the strength of her shell. We couldn't move her without help.

"Tar," I whispered. "We have pretty much everything we need. Let's get the rest of the group and get some help with Ms. Two Ton here."

"Right."

"And don't tell her I called her that," I said.

"Oh no, I wouldn't want to damage that fragile relationship between the two of you," Tar said and smirked. I punched him in the arm and we left the room.

The entire complement of prisoners from the dungeons worked feverishly to lower the ship down to ground level. While we still had the element of surprise, we didn't have an infinite amount of time to finish our task. Given the manpower at his disposal, it would only take a few hours for Zei'Chara and his troops to search the dungeons. With any luck, they wouldn't think to look into this particular hangar section immediately. The Golden Sabre hardly looked like it would fit forty passengers comfortably, much less a hundred. We played the odds that the search party would target the larger cargo vessels first. Still, the clock ticked on and we got closer to being discovering with every passing second. Our group of outlaws and misfits worked quickly and quietly; no one wanted to go back to the dungeons.

I saw Tar pull Dilo aside for a small mission. After a few minutes of instruction, Dilo disappeared with a small box Tar handed to him. Xetoch watched the exchange with great interest, but remained silent. I surmised that Xetoch knew this was Tar's proving ground; he wouldn't interfere or even advise Tar until we reached our destination.

The ship finally came to rest on solid ground after fifteen minutes of Graustish and me frantically manipulating the surrounding machines to end the testing of The Golden Sabre. Five men struggled out of the other room carrying the limp and extremely heavy form of the ship's control link, Kalleen.

"Dang, she's a load!" The Gretn'aak grunted. "Are you certain this particular piece of machinery is really necessary for the job?"

"Without a doubt, she is irreplaceable and absolutely necessary," Tar assured him.

The inside of the ship looked like a science lab had exploded in it. Various lines lay all over the bridge and small diagnostic computers still hummed away near the bow of the ship. Other than an excess of equipment, however, nothing had changed on the bridge. Unfortunately, we couldn't tell what kind of exploration had been performed on the engines or life support systems by the pirates. We only had Tar's cursory external inspection confirming the structural integrity of the ship. After much grunting and groaning, Kalleen finally arrived on the bridge.

Since she was never turned off to begin with, she immediately hummed to life.

"Hello, gentlemen," Kalleen said. "My name is Kalleen and if you would politely put me down, I won't char your hands for touching my body."

"Uh, yes ma'am," the Gretn'aak replied and the others quickly lowered her to the floor of the bridge, glad to give their arms and backs a rest. Red laser light instantly poured out of Kalleen as she checked the ship over.

"Tar," Kalleen said as she walked to the ship's entrance, poking her head out. "The Golden Sabre is completely functional."

She paused and looked at Xetoch.

"Xetoch, you're looking exceptionally well for a man your age," Kalleen said and ducked back into the ship to begin the preliminary launch countdown.

Xetoch smiled as he turned to Tar.

"You know what? She doesn't look a day older than when I last saw her, either!"

Tar genuinely smiled for the first time since we left the dungeons. He became more serious as Dilo walked into the room.

"Xetoch, how long since we left the dungeons?" Tar asked.

"Oh, I'd say somewhere in the neighborhood of two hours. Why?"

"Let's just call it a hunch, but I think we were meant to escape. It's all been just a little bit too easy." Dilo came up to them and raised his eyebrows.

"I planted tha diversion, 'n' then I checked out yer

theory. Ya nailed it."

"Are you sure they saw you walk into that other hangar?" Tar asked. Xetoch frowned slightly.

"They saw me; but, they dinna chase me. They dinna even move in ma direction."

CHAPTER 20
SUICIDAL TENDENCIES

We packed the fugitives from the dungeons into the two cargo bays, three closets, and the bridge, as well as any other nook and cranny that could be found on board The Golden Sabre. For some reason they refused to explain, the three native Telshi chose to remain behind.

"I believe," Xetoch said to me as the Telshi shook hands with Tar. "That they're staying behind because they aren't too keen on sharing space with so many other species."

"I thought they might be anxious to return to their fellow rebel natives," I responded. "Fighting for independence against Zei'Chara must require a very dedicated volunteer force."

"Perhaps," Xetoch said and smiled.

As soon as they said their goodbyes, I couldn't tell the Telshi left because they became immediately invisible to the naked eye. I mused that would be a handy ability to have in most of the scrapes Tar and I found ourselves in.

Tar had enough to worry about without trying to figure out the Telshi. He sat next to Kalleen and stared at the forward screen.

Dilo edged toward him through the crowded bridge. Tar caught sight of Dilo who held up three fingers.

"Kalleen, can you scan the surrounding terrain?" Tar asked.

Kalleen looked at Tar with her metallic eyebrows raised.

"I already have. There are 5,764 buildings, 347,607 large geographical protrusions, and twenty-five hundred large bodies of water."

"Ahem... Just how much of the surrounding area is that exactly?"

"The planet's eastern hemisphere. We are located near the center of it. I am afraid I can do no better than that at ground level; an accurate scan of the entire planet's terrain would require a stationary orbit for a short period of time."

"Right. Um, can you plot us a course to the farthest point from here without going more than a hundred feet above the planet's surface?"

"Tar, it's only a planet. I merely lack a sufficient database to function as an intergalactic navigator. A planet's surface is child's play."

"Good. Do that then."

I pushed my way through the teeming throng towards Tar. A large, ten foot tall being that oozed a slime that smelled worse than anything else I'd encountered provided my only real obstacle. I recalled the challenge we had putting it through the small opening in the dungeon. If it hadn't been for the slime lubricating the way, we would've been forced to leave him behind. He never said thank you. I patted the big, slimy creature on the shoulder as I passed by. At least, I thought I touched its shoulder.

"Tar, do you have any realistic time of departure planned soon? The natives are getting restless."

"Natives?" Tar said. "I thought the Telshi left."

"Actually, I'm referring to our remaining passengers. It's just a figure of speech."

"I wish you'd stop doing that. Terran figures of speech have gotten me into more trouble than I care to admit. We should be departing in approximately two minutes. Kalleen, are you done plotting that course yet?"

"I was finished three milliseconds after you requested it," Kalleen said, holding her chin up.

"Great." Tar looked at me and raised his eyebrows. "Next on your agenda is cutting us a way out of this building. How long will that take?"

"5.8736152 seconds. Is that fast enough for you?" Kalleen tapped her metallic fingers on the chair she sat in.

"Yes." Tar took a deep breath. "Start on my signal... and please round your future approximations off to the nearest second. Thank you," Tar said as he stood up and addressed his full-plus complement of passengers. "Folks, we're gonna take a little trip. Hold onto whatever portion of your anatomy is most dear to you. It's going to be a bumpy ride!"

"Kalleen, keep me informed of any ships that may be in our path," Tar whispered as he sat down.

"Do you wish to be advised of the ones waiting in the air above us?" Kalleen said.

"No, no. I already know about them," Tar glanced at Dilo who held up all eight of his fingers. "Is our path clear now?"

"Yes."

"Then cut away... now!"

Tar hadn't even closed his mouth before light from the forward lasers leapt from the bow and began to cut our way out.

Kalleen cut the exit to the exact dimensions of The Golden Sabre, allowing it to pass through snugly. The final cut loosed that section and it fell to the floor of the hangar with a loud clang. The dust hadn't even started to rise before Kalleen rocketed us out of the hangar. In the ship's explosive wake, all of the monitoring equipment that had been attached to The Golden Sabre a few minutes earlier followed the ship out of the hangar for a few hundred feet.

"I'm not worried about any deaths resulting from our hasty exit," Tar said to me as we climbed into the sky. "Dilo checked out the surrounding area for any personnel that might be in our immediate path. The hangar has some sort of stay clear directive for all of Zei'Chara's troops."

"That's a bit disturbing," I said as I crossed my arms.

"It just confirmed my belief that we had progressed well into a trap very carefully laid for us."

"That doesn't concern you?"

"Not yet," Tar said and winked.

Within one hour, we reached our destination. The Golden Sabre slowed to a stop.

"We have arrived," Kalleen said.

"Wow." Tar took a deep breath. The flight had kept all of the passengers on their toes with sudden dips and bumps. Kalleen compensated slightly for the sake of the passengers so the ride didn't kill them. It was still a little uncomfortable and painful at times.

"Okay. Let's see where our trackers are located."

On the bridge's main screen a tactical display appeared of the southern hemisphere. Blips appeared on the screen showing ships far behind us. One ship several miles above us probably had no idea of The Golden Sabre's location. The other side of the planet showed three small ships appearing, flying faster than the other ships, but at a snail's pace compared to the rate at which The Golden Sabre had just traveled.

"How soon will the ship above us notice we're here?" Tar asked.

"I cannot determine that. It may already know," Kalleen said. "Not that it will matter much. The ship is just a small freighter with no weaponry on board."

"Hmmm," Tar said. "Is there anywhere we can land nearby? Preferably uninhabited?"

"This entire half of the planet is uninhabited; although, that doesn't mean it's entirely safe." Kalleen frowned, an odd look for an android. "Why do you want to land?"

"We have a ship full of aliens of various different species who have not gone to the bathroom for at least four hours," Tar said and looked at a slimy, tentacled alien. "At least I'm pretty sure none of them have gone." He wrinkled his nose and turned back to Kalleen. "We don't have too much time; our 'friends' should be getting close within forty-five minutes."

"43 point... 43 minutes to be exact," Kalleen said as she guided the ship to a landing in a small clearing.

The ship landed and the door opened slowly. Fresh air flooded the bridge. Until that moment, I hadn't fully comprehended just how bad a ship could smell when crammed full of diverse races that sweated in a wide variety of odors and were coated in the collective rotting stench of a city's sewer system. I actually saw a green haze rising from one of our passengers and another moved slightly, popping some kind of epidermal pustule on its head that spurted a thick yellow liquid up into the air. I felt the bile rising in the back of my throat.

Tar stood on the captain's chair and addressed the passengers.

"Okay everybody. Potty break!"

The silence that followed was deafening. The smell hit my nasal cavities like a Nialusian mining cart. Tar squirmed. Finally, Graustish broke the silence.

"Excrement intermission!"

Except for Kalleen, the ship's full complement exited in a matter of minutes.

The surface of Orridon resembled a Terran rain forest, lacking only the lush green color of Terran flora. The plant life was something between a pink and purple shade with sharp, blood red veins flowing through the leaves of the plants. A portion of the group refused to venture forth because they had iron-based blood; the plant life resembled the kind with a taste for red blood. A buddy system solved the problem with incompatible alien species guarding each other's back during the excrement intermission.

As everyone climbed back aboard the ship, Tar watched the surrounding plants warily. As I recalled, he didn't have much experience with blood-sucking plants except for a somewhat harmless, though unnerving incident at the tender age of nine. A small plant had claimed the lives of his clan of pet flohns–a painful lesson in life and death for a nine year old. The plant in question also learned a painful and final lesson. Tar burned it in a quick judgment upon discovery of the flohn skins lying next to the plant.

When Tar thought he had accounted for everyone on board, he closed the hatch, but not before he looked back at the plants one more time and shuddered.

"Some memories are worth forgetting," he said as he made his way through the crowd to the captain's chair.

"Let's hit it," Tar said to Kalleen.

"I take it that you mean 'leave the planet.' But why would you leave one of the passengers behind, especially that nice Fredowurg who's been helping you so much?"

Tar paled. Fredowurgs had iron-based blood.

"Dilo!" Tar called out as he made his way madly to the exit. "Open the hatch!"

I got there before Tar and pressed the button. It slid open, but Dilo was not out there waiting. I shook my head at Tar.

"Kalleen, scan the terrain for him," Tar said.

"I'm afraid that's not possible; the flora in this area emits its own heat. The infrared scan is virtually blocked out, overloaded."

"Damn!" Tar stood next to me and stared out at the surrounding flora. The purple and pink leaves seemed very menacing now. I imagined the leaves digging their way into my flesh and slurping the blood from my veins. With visions like that, I knew I needed a nap.

Tar had a sudden brainstorm. "Kalleen, can you scan for sounds?"

"Yes, shall I scan for his voice?" Kalleen asked as she did it.

Tar thought about it for a moment.

"No. Scan for breathing or struggling, grunting, some kind of sound of someone in stress. He may be tranquilized or poisoned by one of these nasty plants."

Kalleen did so. In a few seconds, she swung around to Tar.

"I've found him approximately fifty feet to the aft of the ship."

"Take us to that spot! Make sure this hatch is facing him," Tar said. He grabbed onto the handles at the side of the hatch for support and kept his eyes on the terrain outside. The ship floated into the air, then lurched as it maneuvered to the spot Kalleen tracked Dilo to. The ship crushed the plants below as it landed at their destination.

Dilo looked up at the hatch as he pulled up his trousers, his face scrunched up into a snarl.

"I dinna suppose ya 'ave any fast acting laxatives aboard that thing, do ya?"

Tar breathed a sigh of relief.

"We'll see what we can do for you on the way. Come on up." Tar reached down and grabbed Dilo's arm; he had to lift him up since there was no room to let down the boarding ramp. Dilo smiled as he got one foot on the edge of the hatch. Then, he suddenly went limp and Tar lost his grip on Dilo's suddenly limp hand. Dilo disappeared into the purple-pink leaves that writhed and swayed like they were caught in a sudden whirlwind. Contrasting with the still air made the scene all that much more frightening.

"Kalleen! We've got to get him back! Can you track him?"

"No, but I can give you something to help you when you go after him." A small panel next to the hatch slid open, revealing a small laser cannon, freshly charged and glowing with energy. Tar grabbed the weapon and leapt to the ground. He disappeared into the bloodthirsty flora. Fift, in a rare departure from translating, jumped out of the ship after him.

As Fift later told us, it didn't take him long to catch up with Tar and Dilo. He heard something fall to the ground a few feet to the right of where he searched and homed in on the laser pistol's resting spot. When he reached them, Tar was unconscious, hanging upside down from a thick vine having a great time twirling Tar like a top. Meanwhile, another vine pulled Dilo into a large opening in the side of a large stem. The opening dripped with a steaming yellow liquid that might have been some kind of digestive fluid. Fift picked up the laser cannon beneath Tar, aimed it at the center of the opening in the stem and fired three short bursts. The carnivorous plant shuddered. The plant tried to find its attacker; but couldn't see him because Fift had copper-based blood. The plant started to pull Dilo closer to the stem opening. Fift fired one more short burst. The plant dropped both of its victims and wrapped its vines protectively around the stem. Fift shoved the laser cannon in his tunic, grabbed Tar and Dilo by their collars, and dragged them back to the ship.

The plant venom wore off in about fifteen minutes. Tar and Dilo woke up to a ship that smelled only slightly better than when they left it. This may have contributed to their retching from the trace of venom still in their system. After a few minutes, they seemed to have recovered from the worst of the venom's effects.

"Kalleen, how much time has passed?" Tar asked, wiping sweat from his forehead.

"According to the Terran calendar, the year is 2413. On the MWGS, it is the 3028th year. The Galactic timetable places us in the year 33106 of the 352nd cycle." Kalleen smiled.

"How much time has passed since we landed?" Tar said as he rolled his eyes.

"34 minutes."

"Thank you," Tar said and bowed his head. "How close are our pursuers?"

"They will arrive in nine minutes," Kalleen said and folded her hands in her lap.

"Thanks." Tar paused to clear his throat and his mind. I remember Rennifej once warning Tar that would be fatal and futile, all at the same time. "Let's give them a few minutes. Then we'll complete the circle."

Several of the passengers shuffled their feet at this statement.

"Circle?" I said.

"Gorth, my friend, I, ahem, that is we are going to make a bold attack on the main palace of Noita Zei'Chara," Tar said.

I felt the blood drain from my face. I opened my mouth, but I couldn't think of a thing to say.

Kalleen cocked her head to the side and frowned at Tar. She placed a single finger on her lips. I thought she would say something, but she remained silent much longer than I thought she would.

Several of the passengers grumbled. Others shushed them.

"Tar," Kalleen said. "You're aware we only have limited capabilities in the weaponry department for planetary bombardment, correct?"

"Of course, but we also have you and me. That combination should be powerful enough to guarantee success in reaching our objective. I believe now would be a good time to get under way. Take us back to the palace, going around the other side of the planet. Best speed, please."

Xetoch listened to what transpired with a keen ear.

"I don't mean to pry," Xetoch said quietly as he walked up to Tar. "But, I don't understand what you're trying to accomplish. Even I can see that this is a suicide mission of the grandest degree. True, a great majority of Zei'Chara's fleet will be detained on the far side of the planet, but you couldn't possibly think that Zei'Chara would leave his palace completely and totally unguarded. I would postulate there are a good two dozen fighter ships guarding his palace, possibly some heftier ships as well. Please consider what I'm saying."

"Are you quite finished?" Tar said. "Unless I'm mistaken, you said you wouldn't interfere or question my decisions from here on out. I'm in command and I don't take kindly to having my decisions constantly questioned. The Golden Sabre will attack. That's my decision. Do we understand each other?"

Xetoch looked at Tar with a bit of confusion.

"You're not quite like the Tar I expected. However, Oedipus' very specific instructions twenty eight years ago to 'get him out of the dungeon and then turn everything over to him' prevent me from taking any other action. Until this morning, the 'him' of the message had not been clear. I'm still not sure of your present state of sanity; but I will follow my best friend's wishes, even if it kills me." Xetoch shuddered and he looked over the crowd of passengers. "Even if it kills us all." He nodded reluctantly to Tar and turned away. He didn't see the tears welling up at the edges of Tar's eyes.

Kalleen beamed her instructions to the ship. She scowled at Tar. It took a lot to get an android angry; you had to work at it. And, even when you got one angry, it was simulated anger or, to be more precise, artificially generated anger, not real anger as live beings know it. Tar reacted to this anger in a most peculiar way.

"Is there a problem with you too, Kalleen?"

"Not anything that a good spanking wouldn't solve," Kalleen said and folded her arms. She turned away from Tar and focused on the view screen.

"Let's just forget the spanking and concentrate on the matter at hand," Tar said. A smile teased the corners of his mouth, but Tar resisted. "What I need you to do is listen closely to my every direction when we're in the upcoming battle. Okay?"

Kalleen paused for a moment. She looked into Tar's eyes. She put her finger on her lips again and tapped them for a few moments. I wondered if this reflected a nervous habit from Tar's flesh and blood grandmother. Kalleen seemed to come to a decision as she placed her hands back in her lap and nodded.

"Very well, Tar. You can depend on my cooperation and support. Do you wish to discontinue hearing advice or counsel from me?"

"Only if it isn't to try and talk me out of this attack."

"Of course."

The ship traveled on.

I strolled up to Kalleen. "So," I whispered, "what's your interpretation of events?"

Kalleen looked at me for a moment. She returned her attention to the view screen and spoke quietly.

"Oedipus had very clear instructions for me before I was put into mothballs all those years ago: 'Do what my grandson asks. Watch him at first, and then let him go.' Now he is finally giving orders on his own instead of taking clues, who am I to pull the rug out from under him? Sometimes, the world throws you a strange curve. If I had been programmed with remorse, I know I would feel it for the rest of the passengers. I know the capabilities of this ship, inside and out. There is no way it will survive a frontal assault on Zei'Chara's palace."

I nodded and smiled grimly. I watched the passengers become more verbal with each other. They snipped and paced as best they could in the confined space they shared. I decided to try my hand at persuading Tar to give up the suicide run at the palace.

"Tar, ol' buddy. I just wonder if you had considered the implications of your actions and the direct result of those said actions," I grinned.

"Not you too." Tar rubbed his eyes. "We are proceeding as planned. Not even you can change my mind."

"But, Tar..." Tar held up his hand to silence me.

"Just trust me on this one. I guarantee you won't be disappointed." He looked at me and smiled. "Trust me, ol' buddy."

The goose bumps permeated every inch of my skin.

Chapter 21
Zip and a Doo Dah

The Golden Sabre zipped through the air only a few hundred feet off the ground. Tar stood next to the command chair where Kalleen kept in constant contact with every system aboard the ship. Kalleen raised her eyebrows as she interpreted the results from the last sensor readings for the area immediately ahead of them.

"Tar, I'm getting some very unusual readings ahead of us."

"There are some ships guarding the palace?" Tar asked.

"There is a thing called an understatement, and you just made it." Kalleen projected her readings up to the main viewer. The main viewer revealed a screen filled with different sized circles, ranging from one-inch to five-inches in diameter. "That is the section of sky directly in front of us. Every circle on the screen represents a ship. I can't accurately portray the entire sky in front of us because of the screen's limitations;

suffice it to say, there is a wall of ships, two and three deep, guarding the palace. I suspect it goes all the way around the palace. Unfortunately, I can't get a more accurate reading; this is well beyond what the sensors were originally designed for."

"I think it's plenty accurate, Kalleen, for our purposes, anyway. Is anything coming up behind us?"

"Yes, three fighters, but they are far behind. I believe they laid in wait before they started their chase. We have quite a head start," Kalleen said as the main screen changed showing the position of The Golden Sabre in relation to the fighters.

"Kalleen, switch it back," Tar whispered. "Don't change the view again unless I say so, okay?"

Kalleen nodded.

Dilo appeared in front of Tar and shook his head.

"Talk to Fift," Tar said to Dilo who left immediately to search for him.

"What's that all about?" Kalleen asked.

"Kalleen, did anybody ever tell you that you ask too many questions?"

"Only your grandfather."

Tar grunted and fixed his attention on the main screen.

"I'm being compared to my grandfather on a regular basis. However, I don't think I'm anywhere close to filling his shoes. Judging from the impenetrable wall in front of us, I believe it would be in our best interests to go to Plan B."

"Retreat?" I said.

"Of course not." Tar grinned. "We're going to attack from above. Kalleen, take us to the vertical zenith above the palace!"

The Golden Sabre responded immediately to Kalleen's wishes. Gravity, being a beastly unforgiving thing, took no mercy upon the passengers aboard the ship. Kalleen complied with a little too much speed.

Tar and I flew backward toward everyone else and wound up on our backs, pressed against the ceiling on one side and our fellow prisoners on the other. Most of the others lost their footing as well, tripped up by gravity and an unusually slick floor. The living pancake piled up on the back of the bridge took on the aspects of a tangle of smelly, squirming sewer worms. Only when the ship reached the zero-gravity effects of outer space did our pile of passengers get some relief and began to move.

"Kalleen!" Tar yelled. He couldn't say much else because he got an anonymous knee shoved under his chin. From my viewpoint, it didn't hurt, it just prevented speech. Tar worked hard to get anything resembling sound past the three layers of passengers above him.

It took about 45 seconds to return everyone to their feet when the artificial gravity took hold. When Tar returned to the command chair, he pursed his lips and frowned at Kalleen. She shrugged her shoulders and smiled.

"You said I asked too many questions. So, I didn't ask any."

"Very cute," Tar said sitting down on the floor and resting his head against the side of the command chair.

I spent a few minutes gathering my wits when I noticed something out of the ordinary. This something had to do with the distance we now were from the planet. According to my mental calculations, the ship should be turned around by now to compensate for our velocity; the longer we waited to turn around, the longer it would take to return to the planet. I looked around the bridge, waiting for someone to point this out. No one did. I judged the surrounding crowd to be more suited to action than to thinking.

"Tar, why haven't we turned around by now?" I kneeled down next to Tar at eye level. Tar grinned.

"Ahhh. You figured that out already? Well, in that case, our friend must be near to the same conclusion," Tar whispered. I opened my mouth to ask who the friend was, but Tar pushed his fingers against my lips, raised his eyebrows and smiled. He grabbed the arm of the command chair above his head and pulled himself to a standing position. "Kalleen, prepare to reverse course. Dilo, are we ready for the attack?"

From the rear of the bridge, Dilo waved a hand in confirmation. Tar smiled.

"Ready at your command, Tar," Kalleen said.

"Fift, fire when ready!" Tar shouted.

Two short bursts of laser fire lashed out from the rear of the bridge near where Dilo was a moment earlier. The shots struck the large, slimy and foul-smelling alien I had patted on the shoulder earlier. The alien's head teetered and then fell to the floor of the bridge with a loud clang. Exposed wires and circuitry spit sparks from the thing's neck; the body shuddered. The thing fell to the floor, pinning several innocent bystanders under it.

We rushed to the motionless, smoking body.

"You appear to have made quite a mess," I said.

As if in response to my statement, the body quivered slightly, making everyone jump, except for the innocent bystanders who remained, quite irritated, under the body. Slowly, the surface of the neck began to rotate like a lid being unscrewed. The pinned, innocent bystanders squirmed and shouted their protests. We readied ourselves for an attack. The 'lid' for the neck popped off and fell to the floor, smashing the pinky finger of one of the innocent bystanders who screamed out in pain and rage. A loud squeak erupted from the neck opening and a small blue alien crawled out; it looked something like a small dragon with horns on its head and a long, powerful tail.

"Oh great," I said with a sigh. "A Zindel." The Zindel leaped at the nearest humanoid, Graustish, and clung fiercely to his hair. I smiled quietly to myself as Graustish attempted to dislodge the Zindel, a feat that few people have been able to accomplish. Zindels had the curious ability to withstand hours of laser fire aimed at them without suffering any ill effects. Aside from their will to cling to a host (the word parasite is much too weak a word to describe a Zindel), the Zindel also had very large claws that persuaded the host to cater to their will. In short, having a Zindel on your back is several times worse than having a monkey there.

Graustish screamed several verbose obscenities which Fift graciously resisted translating. Everyone aboard the ship knew what a curse it was to have a Zindel 'attached'. They were all sympathetic to Graustish's plight, but not to the point where anyone would want to take his place. Tar walked over to the body of the robot and peered inside.

"As I suspected. Run by remote control. The Zindel is merely our 'reward' for subduing the spy robot." Tar helped to lift the robot off of the three people trapped beneath it.

"Kalleen, do you have any ideas for disabling this thing?"

"Throw a sonic grenade in there and shut it tight," Kalleen said as she walked over to the closet we found her in and retrieved a small metallic ball. She tossed it to Tar. "Twist it and toss it in. Then screw the lid on tight. It should shatter most of the circuitry inside."

Tar did as instructed, enlisting the aid of several bystanders to screw the lid back on quickly. A loud 'whoomp' came from inside the robot, lifting it a few inches off the floor of the bridge.

"Well then, let's get the hell out of this solar system!" Tar stepped up to the chair Kalleen had just returned to. "Best speed away from Orridon."

"I'm glad to see my doubts were unfounded. This young hooligan knows what he's doing," Xetoch said to me smiling. I had to admit for today, Xetoch had it right.

"May I ask," I said quietly to Tar. "If you could tell us what we're doing now?"

Tar smiled thinly. "I'm thinking. I'm thinking."

"Tar, my boy," Xetoch said rubbing his hands together. "I have a suggestion, would you care to hear it?"

"Aren't you violating the rules by telling me anything?"

"I think this test is finished for now. Your grandfather may not agree, but then he's not here to tell me otherwise." Xetoch winked.

"In that case, Xetoch, you have the conn," Tar said and bowed to the subterranean master.

"Kalleen, turn us 17 degrees starboard. Then punch it!" Xetoch said, making a punching motion into the air.

"Punch it?" Kalleen glowed as she turned the ship in the suggested direction.

"Give her all she's got. Show those pirates just how fast this baby can go!"

"This baby," Kalleen said and shook her head. "I think I need to brush up on colloquialisms."

Without the restraints of gravity, the ship pushed more thrust through the engines than ever before. The buildup of speed took a few minutes, however. Unfortunately, this gave our pursuers an opportunity to get closer. Our projected path took us uncomfortably close to our opponents, within a few hundred miles, before we reached full velocity and put sufficient distance between us to limit their offensive options. The readouts flashed across the bridge screen identifying potential pirates within range.

"Looks like we got company. Are we going to fly through there fast enough?" Tar looked very concerned. "I'm still not comfortable being responsible for the welfare of a hundred beings."

"It will be close," Kalleen said.

"Well, they're pirates. That means they have very good aim and probably quick ships to boot. You're right. This will not only be close, but too close." Tar paused and thought for a moment. "What if we don't quite push the ship to her limit just yet, and hold back until we're within firing range of the ships? They're aware of our top speed within the atmosphere, but not in space."

Kalleen nodded. "Force the computers to compensate for the wrong speed before firing. That could give us the edge we need."

The Golden Sabre cruised toward the other ships, which began sending messages demanding our immediate surrender. The battleship Shaala gained quickly. I placed my hand over my mouth and felt the sweat forming on my upper lip. That was a lot of firepower breathing down our necks. I wiped my brow and took a deep breath. I looked around and noticed a few passengers clasping their hands together and murmuring.

"Does the phrase 'boxed-in' mean anything to you?" I said as I turned back to Tar.

Two minutes passed before a warning shot came from Shaala. The shot impacted on an asteroid and burned a large crater in the rocky surface.

"I don't think we want to chance this anymore. Hit it, but put that asteroid between us and that monster behind us!" Tar grabbed hold of the command chair as the ship suddenly accelerated and turned. A shot blazed through our former flight path, fading out harmlessly after a few kilometers. Kalleen maneuvered The Golden Sabre into position, using the asteroid as a shield from the battleship's fire, and fired the engines up hotter than they'd been in twenty-eight years. The small outpost ships attempted to attack, but The Golden Sabre went too fast for their weapons systems to track. A few minutes later, the asteroid, now far behind us, shattered from the barrage dealt out by the battleship. The Golden Sabre had pulled out of range and the Shaala could no longer match our speed.

"Whew!" I said and I heard the collective behind me releasing held breaths.

Twenty minutes later, the communication system beeped. Tar and I looked at Xetoch who shrugged his shoulders. Tar opened his hand to Kalleen and she connected the transmission.

The view screen lit up and we saw the Telshi we left behind on the planet.

"That was a wonderful show, Tar. We've never seen Noita Zei'Chara so angry," he said.

"Had a few choice words for his command staff, did he?" I said.

The Telshi shook his head.

"Zei'Chara stormed the palace halls screaming in

anger. Then he used a laser cannon to destroy his own command center."

"Holy," Tar whispered.

"We followed his second-in-command, Krin, as he ran from the command center. He was wincing in pain as he used a communications panel in the palace's foyer to contact the elite guard. He said, 'Keep everyone out of the king's way. This cool down is going to take a while.'" The Telshi grinned. "I believe Krin was nursing a laser pistol wound on his left arm at the time. He rubbed his eyes and left the room in the opposite direction of the destroyed command center."

"Sounds like a job well done," Tar said as he patted Xetoch and me on the back.

The Telshi looked around for a moment and then back at us.

"I must warn you. Zei'Chara swore his revenge before he stormed out of the cindering remains of his command center. I wouldn't take that danger lightly."

"Understood," Tar said and nodded. "Luckily, we spend most of our travels on the other side of the Milky Way, so we won't have a chance meeting anywhere."

"He sent Krin to the medical wing," The Telshi said. "You are not an ally and would not fare as well. Please take care. The reach of Noita Zei'Chara is long and powerful."

"Will do. Thank you," Tar said. The communications link went dark and Xetoch clasped his hand on Tar's shoulder.

"Welcome to life as a true Reztap—powerful enemies will always pursue you."

Tar smirked. "I've been a true Reztap longer than you might think."

The Golden Sabre turned when it reached a certain point, predetermined by Xetoch, then continued on. The ship followed this course for nearly two hours before we reached our target.

To the naked eye our destination appeared to be nothing but a cold, innocuous asteroid floating aimlessly in space. The sensors likewise picked up nothing but a large chunk of worthless rock, although it did list the different minerals inside of the rock.

"Why are we trying to land on an asteroid in the middle of nowhere?" Tar said.

"We're not landing on the rock, my boy. Kalleen, keep going forward. Don't let anything stop you," Xetoch said. "And turn the main screen off, please." The main screen on the bridge flickered into darkness.

Red lights illuminated the interior of the ship.

"Ahh, the fully automated collision warning system your grandfather added to the ship, from the Claché home planet I believe," Xetoch said looking around.

"Won't be getting that serviced any time soon," Tar said.

"Warning. You are about to collide with an unfriendly and immovable object. Please take the proper actions to insure against this," the warning system said. Several minutes passed. The warning continued to repeat until it began a countdown. Our complement of passengers began to grumble again. The Gretn'aak put two hands over his eyes and the other set of arms clasped his hips in a pose that told me he felt unimpressed.

"Collision with unfriendly and immovable object is now imminent. Why oh why didn't you listen to me? Please brace yourselves for impact. 10... 9... 8... 7... 6... 5... 4... 3... 2... 1... Impact." Several of the passengers closed their eyes and cringed. After a few seconds, we heard no tell-tale signs of impacting on the surface of the asteroid. "We have now impacted with the unfriendly and immovable object. Please depart the ship carefully. It's a jungle out there."

Xetoch held up his hand. "Wait for it. All communication on speakers please, Kalleen." After a few breathless seconds, the speakers sprung to life. "Golden Sabre, welcome home. Prepare for docking procedure 12-A. I'll see you all station-side." The voice belonged to Oedipus Reztap.

CHAPTER 22
EXPLOSIVE ENDING TO A NICE VACATION

Kalleen twinkled like a supernova for the next few minutes. The ship maneuvered into place with few complications. Tar paced in the small amount of room available; I'm sure his thoughts dwelled on a 'test.' His lips were set in a straight line. His hands, clasped behind him, moved in concert with each step.

The airlock on the port side of the ship opened with a hiss, flooding the crowded bridge compartment with clean, fresh-smelling air.

"Oh, my word!" I heard Oedipus exclaim over the crowd. He coughed a few times and I think he backed away since I didn't hear him anymore. The fatigued and malodorous passengers made their way off The Golden Sabre. Tar waited for the others to disembark before approaching the hatch. Kalleen followed close behind but remained on board. I confess to having left early with some of the others near the front of the bridge, breaking into a run to take a breath of fresh air.

I moved from the hatch directly into a large room that looked something like a cathedral in size, but very much different in terms of decoration. Frayed ends of conduits, busted pipes and loose wires covered the walls. What appeared to be steel girders hung precariously contributed to the violent, gutted out design. A single chunk of wall betrayed this design. It opened, revealing a clean, well-kept corridor through which all of the Golden Sabre's passengers passed.

I had expected Tar to berate his grandfather the moment he left the ship for the test he endured. However, he just gave his grandfather, who stood as far away from the passengers as he could, a quizzical, bewildered look.

"Hello, Tar. Ah, um..." Oedipus attempted to decipher the strange look he got from his grandson. "They're on their way to the showers; although, it will be quite a wait, considering this station is only equipped with five of them."

"Grandpa, why do the walls appear to be... in a state of disrepair?" Tar asked with his attention focused on what appeared to be a live electrical wire dangling near the floor. Every once in a while, the wire would actually strike the floor and spark.

Oedipus followed Tar's gaze and saw the wire. He smiled and laughed.

"Ah, don't pay it any heed. This whole façade is just that, a charade. A show, if you will, to convince any marauders who might accidentally happen upon the place that it's been stripped of all items of worth. A well put on appearance of a thoroughly scavenged space station, if I may be so bold as to congratulate myself," Oedipus said, leaning on a charred girder sticking up out of the floor of the chamber. Then he jumped forward, startled to see Kalleen looking out of the hatch at him.

"Ah! I almost forgot!" He rushed toward the hatch of The Golden Sabre, reaching into his pocket. When he arrived, he pulled out a small circular device as big around as the palm of his hand and about four inches thick. He tossed it into the hatch, where Kalleen caught it and placed the portable power generator on her left hip.

"Sorry about that, Kal. I should've given that to you a long time ago. But, that might have violated the test's integrity."

"I understand perfectly, Oedipus." Kalleen not only sounded perfectly civil to Oedipus, but she even curtsied for him. Tar rolled his eyes and then took his shot.

"All right, grandfather, why this test? Why go to such great lengths to put me in such a predicament? Couldn't you have accomplished much the same thing with a few words of wisdom, maybe a little impromptu tutoring, or was it absolutely necessary to put my life, my friends' lives, as well as all of the other lives aboard the ship in mortal danger?" Tar built his voice up during his tirade, attempting to reach a shout. Unfortunately, his fatigue combined with the stress of a strenuous escape reduced his speech to a hoarse whisper.

"Why, you ask? Because you're a Reztap, of course! Every Reztap for generations has proved himself in a test of courage, endurance, and leadership! You've just passed yours, by the seat of your pants, but you passed."

"By the seat! How..." Tar cleared his throat and

continued. "Look, I got everybody out of there alive and in one piece; what more do you want?" Tar voice rose.

"You did reconnaissance—those hangars held how many additional ships? Why didn't you get more than one, just in case something happened to The Golden Sabre? What possessed you to take such a big risk with so many lives at stake?" Oedipus laid it into Tar as heavy as he could.

"Well, I... don't know," Tar said, looking puzzled and confused.

"Of course, you don't know! Because you haven't had any formal training. Hell, you probably haven't even read a book on the subject! You did it by the seat of your pants... just like every Reztap before you!" Oedipus positively beamed. He walked over to Tar and hugged him. "Welcome to the family, my boy. You're a true Reztap and 'trouble' is your middle name!"

The corners of Tar's mouth turned up just a bit. He arched an eyebrow and nodded.

"Uh," Oedipus said and coughed as he backed away from Tar. "You smell awful. You should get in line for that shower."

After the showers, everybody slept where they could find a place to lie down. The space station had fifty beds and a few couches the former dungeon dwellers used to their best potential. Even the floor beat the rough conditions they'd lived in for the past months or years. In the relative quiet of the sleeping quarters, no one would have guessed the high level of activity occurring in the two docking bays. Oedipus Reztap and an army of automatons worked throughout the night.

Before his self-hibernation maneuvers, Oedipus had programmed the station's repair facilities and robots to repair two specific ships - The Golden Sabre and Bloated Namreg. He planned every little detail of the test Tar had been put through, down to the repair of the two ships afterward. Although, he admitted the stinky spy aboard The Golden Sabre when she blasted out of Zei'Chara's grasp was a complete surprise. The cleaning took more time on The Golden Sabre than any repairs. He had more time to work on the Bloated Namreg and it had definitely needed it.

Oedipus returned Thadius to his appropriate receptacle, although this oscillated between being returned to The Golden Sabre or being ejected from the station into the harsh cold of deep space. Oedipus' practical joke program took entirely too long to wind down.

Tar awoke as the process of cleaning and repair neared completion. I accompanied him as he searched out his grandfather. This included a lively session of animated insults between Tar and Thadius when Tar decided to search The Golden Sabre for his grandfather. Eventually Tar found Oedipus in the well hidden command center for the space station, which would have remained hidden if Oedipus had not opened the concealed entrance when we passed by.

"I'm a little fatigued and restless all at the same time," Tar said. "All the action I've seen in the last week has left me a little overwhelmed. It was fun and exciting at times, but perhaps a little too much. So, what now, Grandpa? Where to from here?"

"Wherever the stars take you, lad. I'm sure you'll find plenty to do or, in the case of Rennifej, plenty to do will find you." Tar winced at the reminder that Rennifej Bartlett still pulled his strings after so many years. "I know who he is, Tar, but sooner or later you'll have to get that particular monkey off your back if you want to live your own life."

"Monkey?" Tar asked.

"Terran life form. Ask your friend, Gorth, about it. You really should embrace your half-human heritage more." Oedipus waved his hand through the air and shook his head. "The point is you need to take some initiative in getting your own life under control. I admit to manipulating your most recent activities, but I had a good reason. I had to let you see you could take control," Oedipus smiled.

"That was a mess," Tar said pointing behind him.

"Look, Tar." Oedipus folded his hands together. "I had a much different scenario planned for your fifteenth birthday. I knew some really great instructors who would give you the best training. The work I'm involved in puts a lot of resources at my disposal. The best and brightest would've been available to you. Instead, someone threw a wrench into those plans."

"Well, you couldn't have foreseen that meteorite hitting Dad."

"It wasn't an accident. I had contingency plans, other people who could move the plan forward. They were all eliminated in one form or fashion."

"Why? Who would do that?"

"An excellent question. Someone wanted me out of the way for an extended period of time. I have a lot of work ahead of me. Maybe I'll take you to the office one of these days. There is more to our existence than you could possibly imagine."

Oedipus had been planning this little heart to heart talk for the last week. Everything went according to plan until the maintenance robots started the trash compactor. The ill-smelling spy robot had a small, but powerful cache of explosives hidden in a protected compartment; evidently a last resort for Zei'Chara if he could still communicate with the robot.

Oedipus sounded the red alert and left the command center in a hurry, followed closely by Tar. The station shook as concurrent explosions rocked the station. Everyone convened on the haphazard loading dock by The Golden Sabre.

"Tar!" Oedipus shouted above the din. "I hoped to save this for a surprise, but circumstances have prevented it." Oedipus walked over to a portion of the wall and pressed a section of pipe. The entire wall lifted away and revealed the ominous bulk of the Bloated Namreg, loading ramp attached.

"I'm afraid you'll have to take the bulk of the passengers with you, Tar. Let's face it; you've got a helluva lot more room!"

Tar turned to the crowd and shouted at the top of his lungs. "Everybody get a move on! That big yellow ship is leaving very soon!"

The crowd moved quickly up the ramp into the ship, three and sometimes four at a time. Oedipus pulled Tar to the side.

"We haven't got much time left; I have a few things I need to tell you. Your ship is fully operational and slightly modified. Kalleen is going with you; the ship's already set up for it. Also, watch out when you pull clear of the station; there were two or three of Zei'Chara's scout ships snooping around the general area. Looking for you, no doubt. But, they should be following me. Take advantage of my decoy efforts and get to the coordinates I gave to your navigator."

"Navigator?" Tar asked.

"Thadius and I managed to get Chuck repaired. Although, he might have a few personality glitches, we did our best." Oedipus grabbed his grandson in a bear hug.

"Take it easy, Tar, and watch your back."

"You, too. Be seeing you around the galaxy, Grandpa."

After a few minutes the ships closed their hatches with all hands on deck.

The ships fired up their engines as the moorings fell away and the artificial gravity deactivated. The space station started to come apart, but was still intact enough to open the bay doors and allow the ships to leave dock.

Outside the dock, the visual cloaking devices began to fail as they were struck by chunks of steel panel that fell away from the superstructure of the space station. The two ships pulled away from the immediate area. Small explosions continued to rock the space station as pressurized compartments imploded and the fuel reserve tanks breached.

In a matter of minutes, the entire space station was completely destroyed. The explosions propelled debris in several different directions. Shields immediately popped up around both ships, guarding them from damage.

"Shields? When did we get shields?" Tar stood on the bridge of the Namreg now. We looked at a slightly larger view screen than the one I remembered leaving aboard the Namreg. In fact, the whole ship appeared to be somewhat retooled and redecorated; although, judging from the taste, I surmised Chuck didn't do the interior decoration.

"You had them all along, Captain. You just didn't have access to them until now," Kalleen said as she connected to new laser receptors built into the bridge and located throughout the ship.

Chuck walked onto the bridge. His physical appearance hadn't changed, but now he wore a red jumpsuit with black trim. He walked up to Kalleen.

"Kalleen?" Chuck said.

"Yes, and you are?"

"Charles. Navigational android. I've entered both the local and target star charts into the computer. You should be able to utilize them for maneuvers."

"Pleased to meet you, Charles."

"Likewise."

"Chuck?" Tar said.

Charles turned to look at Tar.

"Ahh, Captain Reztap. Pleased to make your acquaintance. If I can be of service, please just ask," Charles turned away and headed for the exit.

"Just a minute, Chuck," Tar said walking after him.

Charles stopped and turned around.

"Do you remember anything before your repair by Oedipus?"

"I'm afraid I don't." Charles shook his head. "Oedipus replaced and upgraded all my memory circuits. I contain a full navigational star chart for all of charted space. I should be invaluable as an asset to this crew."

"Charted by whom?"

Chuck paused for a moment.

"I'm afraid I don't have the answer to that question. If you would like to look further into that information, I would be more than happy to upload everything into the computer, although it may take some time. I believe we're about to engage in some defensive maneuvers which our new passengers may need assistance with."

"We'll catch up later, Charles. Nice to meet you. Welcome to the crew."

"Thank you, sir." Charles turned away but then stopped. "Sir, although it doesn't really make sense, I do have some data in my circuits telling me you prefer to be called 'Rezzy.' Is that correct?"

"Not correct, but interesting that you retain that data."

"Very well, Captain," Charles said.

"See ya later, Chuck!" I said.

"Yes, annoying pipsqueak," Chuck said as he left. He stopped and looked back at me. "I beg your pardon, your name is Gorth. I don't know what came over me."

Charles walked out the exit as Tar walked up next to me and shook his head.

"That's one confused android," Tar said.

"Your grandfather must've taken a few shortcuts to get all this done in the short amount of time he had. I don't think he replaced all those memory circuits."

"More surprises from Chuck." Tar straightened his jumpsuit. "Not looking forward to it."

The Golden Sabre's engines fired up as she headed straight for the pirate scout ships located several hundred thousand miles away. Kalleen maneuvered the Bloated Namreg to head in the opposite direction.

"Kalleen, can you give us a rear view, so we can see how Grandpa's doing?"

"Certainly." Kalleen's laser light dulled briefly. We heard a click and then the sound of metal panels sliding behind us. The picture in front of us remained unchanged. We turned around to see a large rear view screen located in the back wall of the bridge.

"I'm trying hard not to look bewildered every time I turn around in my own ship," Tar said.

The picture on the rear screen encompassed the entire quadrant. The focus adjusted to bring all the ships surrounding Oedipus into view. Four lights dotted the center of the screen, which I assumed to be

The Golden Sabre, the two pirate scout ships, and the remains of the space station. In the far upper left hand corner of the screen four more lights appeared.

"It looks like reinforcements are on the way," I said.

"Kalleen, can we send him a message about those other ships?" Tar asked.

"Captain, that would give away our location to the other ships and waste your grandfather's decoy efforts. Besides, Oedipus Rez has been at this game a lot longer than you have. He knows what he's doing," Kalleen said.

Tar crossed his fingers. The light on the screen which I guessed to be The Golden Sabre stopped moving and remained immobile for several seconds. The other two lights began to converge on it.

"Kalleen!"

"Relax, Captain. The resolution from this distance isn't very good, but my sensors show that The Golden Sabre doesn't appear to be moving because it is headed directly towards us. It will be quite a while before it catches up. The other two ships are in pursuit, as are the ones you saw approaching a few minutes ago," Kalleen paused for a second. "I'm sorry, Captain, but we've reached the target coordinates. We must shut off all external sensing devices at this time." The screens went black.

"What target?" Tar asked.

"We're going back through the trans-warp, of course." Kalleen's lights ceased to emanate from her body. "All external sensing devices need to be shut down to avoid overloading the circuits. The trans-warp is rather destructive to electronic circuitry. You remember what happened to your ship's computer and Charles?"

"Yeah, don't want you winding up like Chuck. Maybe we should warn everybody about the warp before we go through it. It kinda fries people as well as electronic circuitry," Tar said.

"Too late," Kalleen said as the ship began to vibrate violently.

We fell to the floor clutching our stomachs and groaned. We could barely detect yells and cries of distress from others aboard the ship; the wrenching sound of titungsteel superstructure under stress drowned out all but the most distressed of the passengers.

I again experienced the feeling of being turned inside out, an altogether unpleasant feeling. The bridge began to spin, so I shut my eyes. This merely made the darkness behind my eyelids spin which didn't seem to be much of an improvement.

Then it was over.

The forward screen lit up with a glowing circle representing the space warp. Much like you couldn't see a black hole, we couldn't view the actually trans-warp, but instead witnessed the hydrogen atoms flaring in and out of existence around the edge of it.

Kalleen maneuvered the ship to where it wouldn't interfere with any ships coming through the trans-warp. Now we waited. While we waited, however, we didn't get to rest. The various passengers aboard the ship voiced their discontent. Turning inside out is something few people want to experience. For some, it is akin to a very moving, religious experience... a bad, very moving, religious experience. Others might compare it to a milliliter of Lobotomy Slammer; those who experienced more than that rarely experience anything ever again.

"I hope to never encounter a trans-warp again."

Tar sounded calm as he spoke, largely attributed to the fact that he had yet to get up off the floor. I agreed wholeheartedly as I too found a strange sense of calm lying on the floor, just on the brink of vomiting while remaining perfectly still.

"Personally, I think it went a lot better this time around," Tar said. "The air tasted more like candy this time; I believe candy is much easier on the taste buds than copper."

"Well, it doesn't seem to agree with the majority of our passengers. The ones who didn't pass out are emptying the contents of their stomach. It's not going to smell particularly pleasant down there." I shuddered and wiped my mouth with the back of my hand. "I wish I could've passed out like the lucky ones."

Kalleen glowed for a moment. Several small doors in the floor of the bridge opened simultaneously. Small robots floated out of these hatches, hovering about a foot off the floor. Kalleen glowed again, sending the robots on their way.

I watched with wide eyes as the robots floated past me.

"What are those?" I asked as the last one zipped by.

"Cleaning robots," Kalleen said.

"Where did they come from?"

"I'll explain later," Tar said as he rose up from the floor. "Right now, I want to find out how Grandpa is doing."

We all looked at the front screen. It still showed the shimmering halo caused by the trans-warp. This single image persisted for several minutes. Tar found a comfortable place to sit down.

"This is one of the few areas on the bridge which hasn't changed much. Although, I have to admit, the surface of the seat looks cleaner than I've ever gotten it."

Kalleen straightened her shoulders.

"The Golden Sabre should be coming through very soon." Kalleen spoke the words just before Oedipus' ship streaked out of the space warp, narrowly missing us. It spun wildly and left a smoke trail behind it. I turned around and followed the path of the ship behind us on the rear screen. Meanwhile the forward screen lit up briefly like a sun exploding, and then went dark. The faint outline of the trans-warp had disappeared. I turned back to look at the forward screen and observed the front half of a pirate scout ship floating slowly toward us. We returned our gaze to The Golden Sabre attempting to stop its wild spinning.

"Attention unidentified flying yellow orb." The speakers jumped to life jarring Tar out of his seat. Kalleen adjusted the volume and filtered out some of the static followed by several seconds of silence.

"As odd as this may seem, Captain, that is the pirate ship hailing us," Kalleen said. Tar raised his eyebrows.

"Can you aid us, we seem to have lost the tail end of our ship." I recognized Xetoch's voice.

"Kalleen, can they receive us?" Tar said.

"I don't know." Kalleen concentrated briefly. "Go ahead and try."

"Xetoch, how the heck are you?"

The forward screen lit up.

"Just fine, Tar. Did you like that little trick, communicating from the enemy ship? Got the rest of the ships to back off a little with that subterfuge." the picture on the screen was Xetoch, but I saw the bridge of The Golden Sabre behind him.

"Who's in the pirate ship?" Tar said.

"Well, I would imagine a few unlucky pirates. Don't worry, we'll pick them up and deposit them with the proper authorities. Ah, I believe Oedipus has recovered sufficiently to speak to you now."

The haggard face of Oedipus Reztap appeared on the screen.

"Well, I thought I'd fixed that damned trans-warp contraption. Never felt so ill. Damn tricky little devices existing in multiple dimensions, wrangling wormholes. Sorry for the ill effects. I tried adjusting it, but I was too busy to test it thoroughly. Glad to see you made it." Oedipus drank a glowing green liquid from a clear cup. He swallowed it quickly and then grimaced. "Nasty tasting stuff." Oedipus looked to his left briefly and then turned back to face us. "We've got the pirates now. I'll catch up with you at the family reunion, Tar. Good luck, lad."

The screen went dark. Tar stood up and turned to me.

"That's my grandpa! Now, let's get all these people home so we can find that stinkin' scarf!"

The Reztap Chronicles

Book Zero: Mishaps and Mayhem

A Little Misunderstanding

Tar and Gorth are roped into another mission by Renni, Tar's half-brother. This time, they're supposed to make a simple delivery to stop intergalactic war—it doesn't go quite as planned. On top of restarting the centuries-old war between the Clachés and the Progorians, they put their longest serving navigator in a life and death struggle to not get eaten.

Digging Reztap

The seminal story of how Tar and Gorth first met on a rescue mission in a mining colony at the tender age of nine. A girl, two mining carts and a high speed chase that ends with a shocker.

Armed But Not Ready

The latest in a string of mishaps that find Tar and Gorth losing yet another navigator to a tragic circumstance. At an expensive space resort, the dui bail out their latest navigator candidate only to have him fall prey to a girl and her cat. It's like these navigators are wearing red shirts!

Book Two: The Quest for the Insane Moth

As they acclimate to the newly revised ship and crew, Tar and Gorth try to retrieve the scarf lost in the battle with The Insane Moth. Against his mother's demands, Tar drags everyone to the remote and extremely hostile planet of Rimtiki Lumdung. Things seem to be going well as they infiltrate the populace until their plans are thwarted by an old flame of Gorth's—the beautiful and extremely deadly Zeestra.

To escape with their lives, the crew must fight against an ever shortening time line to remove an ancient curse that has plagued the planet for centuries. Will Tar and Gorth live through the ordeal while fighting zombies dead, alive and otherwise? Or will Zeestra's treachery seal their fate and end their adventures forever?